Freak in the Sheets

Freak in the Sheets

CHICK-LIT WITH A TWIST BY

MADAMEK

Q-Boro Books
WWW.QBOROBOOKS.COM

An Urban Entertainment Company

Published by Q-Boro Books

Copyright © 2007 by MadameK

ISBN-13: 978-1-933967-19-6
ISBN-10: 1-933967-19-6
LCCN: 2006936960

First Printing September 2007
Printed in the United States of America

10 9 8 7 6 5 4 3 2 1

Cover Copyright © 2006 by **Q-BORO BOOKS** all rights reserved
Cover layout/design by Candace K. Cottrell
Cover photo by JLove Images
Styling by Rowshana Jackson and Candace K. Cottrell
Editors: Alisha Yvonne, Candace K. Cottrell, Andrea Blackstone

Q-BORO BOOKS
Jamaica, Queens NY 11434
WWW.QBOROBOOKS.COM

Dedication

For all the ladies in the streets and freaks in the sheets.

Acknowledgments

Thanks to God for seeing me through each and every time. To my family, I do it all for you.

To D.F., you know I love you. You really are my knight in shining armor, and even though I drive you crazy, I know you feel the same. As you told me, we are about to take over the world!

To Mark and Sabine, thanks for putting up with me. You have allowed me to grow and prosper. To Candace, thanks for helping me out all those late nights.

Special thanks to the staff and authors of Q-Boro, Urban, and Kensington. D. Mitchell, thank you for your help. I'll see you at the top!

To T.C.R. thanks for being my sounding board, friend, and cheerleader. You are appreciated more than you know.

To Andrea, thanks for the encouragement.

Visit MadameK, Layla, Raquelle, and the whole gang on-line at www.FreakIntheSheets.com.

Prologue

Somewhere in Washington, D.C.

Two women were parked in an ice silver Bentley in a dark alley.

"I'll give you fifty thousand dollars if you get rid of her," the driver said, handing a small vial.

The passenger, a much younger woman dressed in a Versace hoodie, Parasuco jeans, and Nike Shox took the vial and thought for a moment while twisting her finger around her ponytail and snapping her gum. After a few minutes of this, the driver grew impatient.

"Do we have a deal, young lady?"

The young woman stopped her fidgeting and looked at the driver, taking in the woman's opulent jewelry and tailored suit.

"Seventy-five gees and we have a deal." She placed the vial in her front jeans pocket.

The driver mumbled obscenities under her breath before agreeing.

"When?"

"Don't worry about that, lady. I got this shit on lock. But I'mma need 45 gees up front, though."

"Tomorrow. I'll meet you here at seven-thirty."

"Bet that. And don't be late. I got shit to do."

The young woman exited the Bentley and walked out of the alley. There was a white Excursion waiting for her around the corner. When she tapped on the window, the man unlocked the doors and she climbed in.

"We got a deal," she said to the man. "Now we gotta figure out how we gonna do this." She pulled out the vial and showed it to him.

The young man turned to his woman and said, "Don't worry. We got this, baby."

Chapter 1

Raquelle

Being a librarian definitely had its benefits. I was able to read when things were slow, and in the course of the five years I worked there, I was able to combine my two passions—reading and sex. Now don't get it twisted. I'm not a slut, a ho, a promiscuous girl, or a prostitute. I'm a lady in the streets, but truth be told, I'm what some would call a freak in the sheets.

When you don't have a man to practice your techniques on, you really get to know your body and what turns you on. I was on a two year hiatus from dating, and let me tell you, I knew exactly what me and my pussy wanted.

As a matter of fact, I was able to earn my degree in Human Sexuality by taking night and online classes while I worked at the library. I liked having access to research materials, but there were times when I wanted to put my sexual research into muthafuckin' practice. However, I had grown out of one night stands and fucked up relationships, so I wasn't going to jump into anything. Or let anything jump into *me*, if you know what I mean.

I was in love a few times, but it turned out messed up each and every time. I won't lie; I had some part in the demise of the relationships, but mostly, the men just didn't get it.

Take my ex-boyfriend for example. Evan Andrews was a fine, Tyrese-looking brother, and he was good as gold to me. He made me come every time and treated me to nice dinners and trips (which I wondered about because his ass was a mechanic at a Dodge dealership). He claimed he was doing side work for some of the customers off the books. Oh, it was off the books, but it was more chronic being exchanged than transmission fluid.

His dumb ass got locked up for three years. At first, I stood by him, wrote him, sent him books, and deposited money his account every month. But after a while, I started thinking I was the one getting played. So I stopped the visits, the letters, all of it. I thought he had gotten the hint that I was done with his dope-selling ass, but he kept sending me letters and calling my cell collect until I got sick of the shit and changed my number. Once a week, I'd send back all his letters "return to sender." He never stopped writing, and I bet the poor muthafucka who got my old cell phone number can attest that he didn't stop calling either. I moved to Northwest DC from my place in Bladensburg, Maryland about a year after he got locked up, and I honestly thought I would never see him again.

I dated a little here and there after that, indulging in some of my sexual desires, but that got old too. Again, none of them really got it. They were either too damn clingy or bigger dogs than Snoop. So, one day I woke up and decided

I was going to stop depending on a man to fill me. Pun intended, dammit.

I was jaded on the love front, due to a bunch of assholes running in and out of my life, but another part of me wanted that shit Mary J. talks about. I wanted to be so sprung on someone I couldn't "be without cha, baby."

There was one man who I felt could get me that sprung. His name was Lucas Lane, and he was a fine, Maxwell-meets-Boris Kudjoe-meets-MosDef kinda brotha. Oh, and my best friend, Layla Lane, happened to be his little sister.

Me and Layla had been friends since junior high. My mom and I moved from New Orleans to the DC area to start fresh after Mason walked out on us. No, he wasn't my father, nor was he my stepfather. He was just some guy my mom liked.

Anyway, I met Lucas the first time I was invited over to Layla's estate to spend the night when I was about fourteen. That was thirteen years ago, and although we had made eyes at each other, flirted, and joked around, nothing ever came of it. I think part of the reason why we never pursued each other was because of Layla. I didn't want it to be any weirdness between me and her if things didn't work out with her brother. I can't say why he never really kicked it to me, but I suspect it was for the same reason.

Can I be honest for a moment when I tell you that my purple (silicone of course) vibrator was named Lucas? Part of me felt like I was preparing for the day when he was entering me and I would gasp his name in the throes of passion. But it was just a fantasy. One I happened to think on when things were slow at the library.

The library was a dull place to be the Friday afternoon before all hell broke loose. My bright fuchsia and orange skirt and my reading material were the most exciting things in the place. I was leaning on the circulation desk, reading the latest book that had come in on multiple female orgasms with one eye and watching over the computer tables with the other. The regulars were all there; furiously updating their MySpace pages and checking craigslist before their thirty-minute time limit expired.

I always knew when one of them hit a site that was supposed to be in the restricted list, but was somehow overlooked by the computer techs. They'd get that look on their faces as if it was their birthday and Jenna Jameson just jumped out of their cake. That's when I'd make my rounds to discreetly look over their shoulders, shake my head, and suck my teeth in disgust, causing them to quickly close the browser window, pack up, and run out of the place. That's if I was lucky.

Some of the regulars had gotten pretty bold. They'd just go about their business until I called them out.

"Jericho, why are you looking at that site? This is supposed to be a place of education, and I can't believe you're using the computers provided by taxpayers' money to look at—"

"Oh, I clicked on here by accident, Rocky."

"Mmm-hmm."

That day, though, I hadn't had any run-ins with the porn pirates to keep me awake after my Mexican fiesta of a lunch. I was a little bored until the phone rang and scared the shit out of me.

"Raquelle, can you hear me? I walking back to the office and it's loud as hell out here. These jerks are trying to run me over." Layla's voice competed with traffic and other obnoxious city sounds.

"Good God, woman, don't you know a library is a quiet place?" I tried to whisper, but it came out louder than I hoped. All the regulars froze and looked up at me. I waved them off.

"Whatever. Look, I need to get out tonight. Lucas's band is playing at Takoma Station at nine—Bastard, can't you see me crossing the street—anyway, you game?"

All she had to do was mention her brother's name and my face got hot. I was more game than Milton Bradley, and the icing was the tequila I'd be inhaling.

"You know this." I looked up and saw Jericho approaching the desk with a couple smutty romance novels from the shelves. I ignored him.

"All right then, I'll swing by your place around eight with some supplies so we can get the party started a little early."

"Bet," I confirmed.

After hanging up, I returned my attention to Jericho, whose leathery face had taken on a sinister smile. He was trying to read my orgasm book upside-down.

I grabbed the romance novels from his hand and said, "OK, Hot Pants, give me your card."

His eyes never left my book until my jailbird ex-boyfriend, Evan Andrews, came rambling through the door and yelled, "There you are. There's my ma'fuckin' baby."

The books I had in my hand dropped to the floor, as did my mouth.

Chapter 2

Layla

"I understand, Mr. Tilley, but at the same time, the return on investment just isn't worth the risk." I plugged in my headset because my neck was starting to ache from trying to talk him out of investing in a fly-by-night tech stock.

My father walked in my office and his tall, lanky frame loomed over my desk while he rubbed the salt and pepper hair of his neatly trimmed beard. One of his cufflinks caught a ray of light coming through the window behind me and nearly blinded me. I put my hand on my forehead to shade my eyes and continued my explanation to Mr. Tilley.

After I hung up ten minutes later, my father finally sat in the navy blue visitor chair in front of my desk and said, "You could've handled that better. You know Mr. Tilley is one of our premiere clients."

I sighed. I felt like I'd been admonished for forgetting to feed the dog. "Yes, Daddy, I know. But he wasn't trying to listen to reason."

I'd been working at my father's investment firm since I

knew how to use a calculator. I thought after getting my masters in finance, he'd show me a little more respect and ease up off me a little, but I was mistaken. In fact, things seemed like they'd only gotten worse. I knew my father was concerned about the reputation of the firm and keeping the clients happy, but I'll be damned if he wasn't driving me crazy in the process. I wondered if he ever did any of his own work or if he just breathed down the necks of the associates all day.

"Layla, dear, you know as well as I do that we have to keep our clients happy. The best way to do that is to keep them rich."

I dropped my head a little. "The only reason he wants to invest in that company is his son-in-law owns the place. The company has no strategy for answering to the new software release by its competitor."

My father stood. "Well, then it's your job to make sure he understands that." He turned to leave.

"That's what I was trying to do," I mumbled.

"What was that?"

"A great day to you, Daddy."

"Hmph."

After he closed my door, I could see him stop at my assistant, Lynette's desk. Lynette gave him her undivided attention. I could see she'd placed a call on hold to listen to Daddy. Her too-white teeth gleamed in his face as she threw her long weave over her shoulder. My father's eyes crinkled from the charming smile that was plastered on his face when she spoke. I didn't remember him ever smiled that hard at me in the office.

I was so sick of the job, the company, and all of it. I knew there had to be something better for me out there, but I was a prudent, careful thinker and planner. I was twenty-seven years old and I already had enough money from investments, saving, and commissions to retire. However, I continued the daily grind, trying to get more.

I was actually afraid that if there really was something better out there for me, I'd be too blind to see it if it smacked me in the face. I was stuck in a rut and I didn't know how to get out of it.

I perused my email for a while until my father left Lynette's desk. As soon as he was out of sight, I shut down my computer and started packing up my stuff to get the hell out of there.

Thank God for Raquelle Scott. My girl definitely knew how to get your mind off things you didn't want to think about. When I arrived at her apartment, with tequila and mixers in tow, she opened the door and Missy Elliott's "Beep Me 911" surrounded my senses.

"What's good?" Seeing the solemn expression on my face, she added, "Just what's good. Not what's bad, what's medium, or what's so-so. Let's make this night what's good."

I nodded and she grabbed my hand and sat me down on her burgundy sofa while she nearly skipped into the kitchen with the bag I had in my hands. Her long, wavy, mahogany hair bounced along with her. At that moment she reminded me of Jennifer Freeman, the daughter on *My Wife and Kids*. Raquelle had a youthful demeanor to her that drew people, including me, to her.

Missy and 702 started to lift a little bit of the tension that had made its home in my head since my father walked in my office earlier that day. I leaned back and kicked off my brown stilettos to let my dogs have a break.

Raquelle came out with two margaritas. She shook her rump to Missy, and handed one of them to me. She did one more twirl, making her red and yellow ethnic printed miniskirt swoosh, and then sat down next to me.

"Whew, if you only knew the shit that popped off at the library today." She slowly shook her head as if she still didn't believe what had taken place. "But let's not go there. I just wanna have some fun and drool over your fine-ass brother." She examined her medium-length nails, which were painted the same color red as her skirt and long sleeved tee.

"OK, now you have me wondering. I know you said only 'what's good,' but the suspense is killing me." I giggled.

"You won't believe me if I told you." She sighed and leaned back.

"If you don't stop skirting me, I'm going to give you the dreaded nipple twister."

We both cracked up, remembering our days as teens when we'd fight over clothing and makeup and would end up in a wrestling match. The nipple twister was always my deal-breaking move.

"Heffa, I wish you would. You know I been doing kick-boxing and you don't want to mess with Rocky."

I laughed as she jumped up and did a boxer's dance before giving in and sitting back down.

"OK, OK. But you still ain't gonna believe it."

The frown on my face told her to continue.

"You won't believe who showed his convict ass at my job."

"Oh, no."

"Oh, yes. And do you know he was up in there hollering and cussing like he was at a fuckin' football game?" She rolled her eyes and took a big gulp of the green drink.

"So what did he want?"

She emptied and put her glass down so hard it made me flinch. "Umph. He wanted to know why I had stopped writing him, wanted to pick things up right where we left it before his dumb ass got locked up."

"He still thinks you're together? You can't be serious."

"As a heart attack. I'm ride or die, but only if you aren't caught up doing something stupid like selling some fuckin' drugs. Shit, if he would have been locked up for defending my honor or a bar fight gone wrong, I might have considered holding him down. But selling drugs when you have skills like fixing cars? Fuck that. That's just lazy. Oh sure, I stood by him for a while. But then common sense kicked in, and it just didn't seem worth it."

"Yeah, but you loved him." I couldn't help but bring that up. That was the one thing lacking with my fiancé, Hunter and me. He was a doctor, had the looks, had the money, but I wondered if he was really right for me. I definitely cared for him, but I didn't feel any kind of spark. Not like the one I used to see when Evan and Raquelle were together. Or the one she got in her eye when I mentioned my brother's name. I was almost sure that was only an infatuation-type crush, though.

She looked at me and said nothing for a moment. "Whoa-oh-oh, what's love got ta do, got ta do with it?" Raquelle sang and she got up. "Girl, get your head out of the clouds and those romance novels. Anyway, let me go finish my make-up so we can get out of here."

I nodded, even though her skin already looked flawless and her eyelashes couldn't get much longer without it looking like she was going for the drag queen look. I sat there while Raquelle sang an almost perfect rendition of the Tina Turner anthem in the bathroom.

". . . got ta do with it?"

"A lot," I whispered to myself.

With that, I sighed and made a quick call to Hunter.

"Hey, baby," he answered.

"Hey you. I just wanted to let you know that I'll be staying with Raquelle tonight. She and I are going to hear A-Train at Takoma Station."

"A-Train? Is that Lucas's new band?"

"Yep. They're moving more toward the jazzy R&B vibe now."

"I see. I wish I could join you, but I'm over here knee-deep in study materials. I only have three more weeks before my exam."

"Right."

"Have a good time, though. We'll link up tomorrow."

"OK, babe."

"Love you."

I cringed a little. I hated saying it for some reason, but I guessed that Hunter was as close to love as I was going to get.

"Love you too."

Chapter 3

Lucas

Catalina was working my last nerve. Not only had we spent two hours arguing about what I should wear for my gig at Takoma Station, but now she was sitting at a table, giving me the evil eye as I spoke to the lovely sound engineer, Kiley. Catalina thought every woman I spoke to was a threat to her queendom. I took a healthy sip of my Heineken, trying to calm my nerves, which Catalina had so effectively trampled on.

Actually, I'd come to the conclusion that anything that even smelled like fun was on Catalina's no-no list. Take our sex life, for instance. After being together for two long years, this woman still refused to lick the stick or do anything outside of the missionary position and me licking the kitty. Yeah, it was still better than spanking the monkey myself, but damn. Can't a brother get some spice in his life?

Catalina gave me and Kiley a mean look, dialed a number on her pink phone and stomped off to the ladies' room in a pink blur. The girl wore pink so much, I'd come to wonder if she was a spokesmodel for Pepto-Bismol. I had to draw the line when she tried to put some pink sheets with dark pink flowers on my bed. She got mad and pouted for a while, but I couldn't go out like that. No respectable man would allow a woman to do that shit.

"What's wrong with her?" Kylie asked as she unwrapped some mic cords.

"I wish I knew." I polished off the last of my beer and finished setting up the drum mics for Raleigh, my talented, but always late, drummer.

After about twenty minutes, the rest of the band showed up and people started trickling in and filling up the tables. There was still no sign of Catalina, and I was indescribably at ease. I started playing some well-known jazz tunes on the piano while I waited for show time.

I saw my sister and her girl Raquelle come in and take one of the reserved tables. Raquelle was looking like a black bohemian superstar with her colorful dress, big earrings, and long, wild hair. She smiled at me and I nodded my head and winked at Layla while my fingers tickled the keys to the tune of Duke Ellington's classic "In A Sentimental Mood" with a fresh, updated tempo. That was part of A-Train's hook and one of the reasons I think our shows were so well attended. We took the classics and brought them into the present.

Catalina finally showed up again, with her minion Sierra in tow. I assumed Catalina had contacted Sierra when she disappeared. Catalina couldn't stand to be seen anywhere alone; I sometimes wondered if she called Sierra over to watch her play solitaire.

Sierra was definitely a cutie, but there was something off

about her besides the fact that she acted as though Catalina were her mother. She rocked the Eve-ish blond hair, and she always dressed to the nines, but she never looked quite comfortable. Kinda like someone else laid out her clothes and told her to put them on.

I couldn't complain too much, though. Sierra gave Catalina someone to boss around when we weren't together.

The guys finally made their way to the stage, and we rocked our first set. I kept thinking about how sexy Raquelle looked when she'd down a shot of tequila and suck on the lime, but I couldn't be too obvious about my fascination. Catalina would act a damn fool if she caught me making eyes at anyone.

I headed outside during the break to get some fresh air and re-center myself. When I stepped out the door, I saw Raquelle down the sidewalk on her cell phone having an argument with someone.

"No, it's *not* the same. You're not the same; I'm not the same. Nothing is the same." I could smell the scent of cloves as she inhaled and exhaled a drag from her smoke. "I'm not going to do this now." She closed her phone.

I felt like I was intruding, and turned to go back in, but when I did, Catalina was staring me in the face.

"And just what is going on out here?" she asked.

Raquelle turned around and looked surprised to see us both. She dropped her clove cigarette on the ground and twisted her red stiletto to stomp it out.

"Oh, hey, guys. I was just out here getting some air." Raquelle winked.

Catalina's face remained twisted. She sucked her teeth and grunted.

Raquelle patted me on the bicep. "Great show so far," she said before going back inside.

"You better leave that black-hemian trash alone," Catalina said after Raquelle had disappeared.

"What? I wasn't even talking to her."

"Whatever." And the pink blur went back inside.

I just sighed and headed to the bar. Raquelle and Layla were at the bar refilling their drinks. I went over to where they stood and grabbed the back of Layla's shoulders.

"Take it easy, sis. We don't want you to get too tipsy now." I grinned.

"Whatever," she replied then tipped the bartender and turned around to face me. "It's all about me and these appletinis tonight."

"We got a cab here, and we're getting one back to my place, so don't worry." Raquelle turned around with her tequila gimlet in her hand and smiled. "I hope I didn't get you into any trouble out there." She nodded toward the entrance.

"Don't worry about that. You weren't doing anything wrong. Catalina can be a little bit . . ."

"A little bit what?" I heard Catalina snap from beside me.

Catalina startled Raquelle so much she splashed some of her drink directly on Catalina's baby pink top.

"You piece of trash!" Catalina looked down.

"Who you calling trash, you siddity bitch?" Raquelle countered.

Catalina shoved Raquelle, but Raquelle threw the first smack. Catalina came back with a hair-pulling move and that was when I heard someone scream. Everyone formed a circle around us, trying to see who was going to win the catfight.

Somehow, I ended up on the floor staring up Raquelle's skirt as she cold-cocked Catalina straight in the jaw.

I saw Layla stand there for a moment before she got her wits and grabbed Catalina from behind.

"Are you crazy? What's wrong with you?" Layla asked.

Catalina released a warrior cry and elbowed her in the stomach.

"You're out of your mind if you think I'm going to let that go. Raquelle touched her friend's shoulder before doing a wild kickboxing move and knocking Catalina flat on her behind.

Layla took that opportunity to pin Catalina down and I rolled over, stood up, and grabbed Raquelle around the waist (which I have to say, felt good as hell).

Elliott, the big, burly bouncer, saw everything, including the fact that Catalina started the mess. I walked Raquelle and Layla over to a table and told them to sit there until I came back.

I spotted Sierra coming out of the ladies' room, looking all around like she was lost. Then she spotted the aftermath, her face twisted up in what looked like a combination of embarrassment and anger, and took off past me. It seemed like she had missed the whole thing.

When I turned around, I saw Elliott escorting Catalina out of the club with Sierra following behind her. I heard her ask Elliott what was going on, but then they were out the door and out of earshot. Red would have been a more appropriate color for Catalina at that moment.

The nagging voice in my head returned. It had been there since I proposed to Catalina last year. My family and society told me it was the right thing to do—that we had been dating long enough and the next logical step was to get married.

I knew from a young age that wanted a family, including a few kids, so the idea of marriage didn't really daunt me. The idea of marrying Catalina, however, did.

I pushed the voice out of my head and refocused my attention on Layla and Raquelle. I went over and told the bartender to keep their drinks coming before I headed back to the stage to finish out the night.

After another set and a half, I looked out to see Raquelle and Layla getting ready to leave. I winked at Raquelle and she blew me a kiss. I got a little twitch in my groin when she turned around to walk out.

Maybe Catalina does have a reason to worry, I thought.

Chapter 4

Evan

Ay, you know how you sometimes feel like shit is falling down all around you, and you're just waiting to get knocked in the head with some debris or some shit? Yeah, well, that's how I felt when Rocky told me to get lost when I showed up at her job.

See, I was hoping that me and her would be together once I got out of lockdown. Matter of fact, I dreamed about the day I would be released every day of the three years I was upstate. I visualized me walking out the prison to my baby waiting in the car. I dreamed about her taking me home and putting her thang on me and then cooking up some of her jambalaya. It's funny, though. I never really got past that part of the fantasy.

Rocky probably thought I was a dumbass for getting locked up for selling weed, but what she didn't understand was that I was doing it for her. I wanted to take her nice places and give her nice things, but I couldn't do that on a mechanic's salary.

Now don't get me twisted; I'm not blaming her. I'm just saying, she makes a brother wanna do her right. Rocky was the kind of girl that dudes talk about when they say wifey. Just knowing she was waiting for me on the other side of those walls kept me sane in there.

The girl was beautiful beyond words with her Creole looks and her thick lower half. Her hair used to make females whisper about her, talking bout that shit can't be real. It fell clear down her back in perfect waves and when she was standing in the sun, it had almost a golden tone to it.

The thing that used to get me, though, was her skin. She was airbrushed in real life. When I was locked up, I used to look up at her picture and imagine I was touching that silky skin. It was the color of a cup of coffee with extra cream and it was just fucking flawless.

When the letters started coming back as "return to sender" and the house phone I was calling her on got cut off, I knew something wasn't right, but I couldn't put my finger on what it was. I just knew she wasn't laid up somewhere with another dude while I was doing my bid. That just wasn't her style. I had one of my boys on the outside keep an eye on her to make sure she was safe. He came back and told me she wasn't seeing anyone, but was going to night school by herself. I told him to make sure she got there and home safe.

I loved that girl, but I thought it was pretty messed up that the last three years of my life were spent in a fuckin' hell hole and she couldn't hold me down. Ay, I know it was a stupid reason to get locked up, but, damn.

My mama held me down, though. She came to visit me every other week for the first six months I was locked up. Then, I got a letter from her telling me that at just fifty-six years old, she had brain cancer and the doctors were giving her three months to live. They didn't want her traveling too much, and she was in a lot of pain. She did make it up there one last time, though. I'll never forget that conversation.

She looked wore out, but she smiled anyway. "Evan, there are some things I want you to know before I die."

"Ma, you ain't gonna die. You still young."

"Baby, I appreciate you saying that, but they's some business we need to tend to." She shifted in her seat.

I still didn't want to face it, but I nodded.

"I'm leaving the house and half my assets to you. Now, before you say anything, I've already told your brother. He wasn't happy about it, but I can't worry about that. You've always been there for me when I needed you, and even though you made some bad choices, I know you a good man."

I felt like I was going to cry, but I just sniffed and manned up.

"Now, Evan, I want you to find you a good woman and raise you a family. I want you to give your kids something I couldn't give you and your brother. A father."

I promised her that day that I would carry out her wishes.

At the funeral, my brother Russell didn't even look at me. I wanted to yell at him that we were the only family we had left, but I ain't wanna disrespect my mama's homegoing like that. I haven't talked to Russell since, and that was like two years ago.

When I got released, my mama's words were echoing in my head, so the first place I went was to get my woman.

When I went to Rocky's job that morning after I got released, I was hoping she'd see me and everything would go back to normal, but I guess I was dreaming. She basically played me out in front of everyone and told me to bounce. I called her job later that night and told them I was her brother from Louisiana and misplaced her cell phone number. Those dumb muthafuckas gave me the number, but when I called, I could hear music in the background and she wouldn't talk to me. I was starting to get salty, but I felt like I had to keep hope alive and shit.

I went to my mama's house, which was now my house, after leaving Rocky's job and started setting up shop.

One of the first things I bought with the money mama had left in a bank account with my name on it was a computer, printer, iPod, internet service, a bunch of CDs, and all the accessories. I wanted to use the computer for looking for jobs and learning the things I had missed out on while I was away. I started my plan by doing a job search in the area for mechanics. I printed out a couple that looked like something. I also did some research on learning how to repair foreign cars, since there was way more money in that than the American stuff. I looked up a few training programs and printed out the information.

I was hooking up my iPod with some of the new music I bought. It took me like three hours to figure out iTunes, but I got it and was rolling. While I was arranging my playlists, I got the idea to make Rocky a mix CD of all the songs we used to listen to together. I wanted her to remember that we had good times together and that we were in love. Real love.

Chapter 5

Raquelle

That shit at Takoma station had me fuming like a mofo. I got a little drunker, as did Layla, and we called a cab before Lucas was wrapping up the last set. I waved goodbye to him and blew him a kiss before following Layla outside. When we got to my house, she called me on it.

"What was that little kissy-kiss for?" She flopped down on my couch, laughing her ass off.

"You're the funniest person you know, aren't you?"

"No, you are," she said as she continued to laugh.

I waved my hand at her. "Damn siddity folk. Dress y'all up, can't take your asses nowhere. Who would have thought, Miss Priss could throw a mean right hook?" I rubbed my cheek.

Layla laughed. "You think it was mean tonight, wait until tomorrow. You know drunk people can roll with the punches, but when they wake up . . . whoa."

"Shit. Don't remind me."

I went into my bedroom to undress, and within minutes, heard Layla snoring softly on the couch. I got under my sheets and took a deep breath. By the time I was finished exhaling, I was out cold.

The next morning, Layla and I made some waffles and coffee and ate while watching some HGTV. Between the two of us, our homes had seen more makeovers than the Lancôme counter at Macy's.

I walked her out a little after noon, and as she was driving off, I peeked into my mailbox. The postman had left me a new DVD from NetFlix and a bunch of bills I wanted nothing to do with. Under all of that, was a CD in a blue jewel case with the word REMEMBER written on the front.

I got a weird feeling in the pit of my stomach. My first thought was that it was a bomb or something, but then I thought who would make a bomb out of a CD. The writing on the jewel case insert looked familiar, but I couldn't place it. Curiosity got the best of me, so I went inside and dropped the mail before walking over to my stereo. I took out my new Tamia's latest out of the changer and replaced it with the one that was left for me in the mailbox.

I pressed play and Amel Larrieux's voice came over the speakers, singing "Make Me Whole." I instantly knew Evan had left the CD and wanted to get up to turn it off, but my body wouldn't allow me to. I sat there through the song with tears streaming down my face, remembering when Evan told me I made him whole. I moved to get up, but when I heard Maxwell singing "Fortunate," I fell back. I was instantly transported to the night Evan and I first made love and this song came on the radio while we were lying there in the afterglow.

I sat there while the entire CD played, each song bringing back good memories. When the last song played, "Back At One," I picked up my pocketbook and rummaged around until I found my cell phone. I looked at the incoming calls from the night before until I found his number.

It took me about ten tries to work up my nerve to call, but I finally connected.

"Rocky? Is that you?" Evan asked just after answering.

"Yeah, it's me."

"Did you get the CD?"

"Yeah, I got it. Look, Evan. I think we need to talk."

"I agree."

"Meet me at the spot Monday night at 5 P.M." I wanted to see if he still remembered where my favorite restaurant was.

"Bet. Paco's in Georgetown Monday at 5 PM."

Impressive.

I turned the CD back on and set it to repeat. For the next two hours I lounged in my spa tub, reheating the water as needed. I cried. I cried for the love I had for Evan. I cried for the love I had for Lucas. I cried for the pain I caused Evan. I cried with a purpose.

Once I was wrinkly from soaking and my tear ducts had seemingly dried up, I got up and watched movies for the rest of the day. Even the next day, I was in a funk I couldn't snap out of. I couldn't stop thinking about the meeting with Evan. I didn't know what was going to happen when I got there, but I knew I had to go.

Chapter 6

Catalina

"Get your dirty hands off me," I screamed, twisting out of the burly bouncer's grasp.

He let go. "Don't come back around here. You're not welcome."

I turned to Sierra. "Hmph. Can you believe that fool?"

"Cat, you can't just go around starting fights. What was that all about anyway?"

"That common hoochie was trying to steal my man, you idiot." Sometimes I had to spell out everything for Sierra. She was such a child.

Sierra's parents and my parents were friends since my father and her father were at Howard together. Our mothers are friends as well, and so it was natural that the two of us would become close. However, sometimes I rethought my decision to associate with her. It was such a chore.

"Who?"

I rolled my eyes. "Rachel, Layla's friend."

"You mean Raquelle?"

"Whatever."

I followed Sierra to her little Lexus SC, which I loathed. The thing was smaller than a soda can.

"Really, Sierra. This car . . ."

"Would you just shut the fuck up and get in the car?"

My mouth gaped open. *Did she just curse at me?*

"I don't know what has your panties in a bunch, but I suggest you—"

"What? What the fuck are you going to do? Look, either get in the car or I'm leaving your troublemaking ass here."

I didn't feel like getting into a filthy taxi, so I just shut up and got in.

"Can you believe that common bitch?" I asked as we drove toward Wisconsin Avenue.

"Whatever, Cat."

This was too much. I couldn't understand why she was speaking to me so harshly. "Can't you see I am having a serious crisis?"

"One you created, as usual." Sierra looked at me, raised her eyebrows and then refocused her attention on the road.

I gasped. "What did you say?"

"Nothing," she said.

"Anyway, I think we need to come up with a plan. I want Layla and that common bitch she runs around with to pay for embarrassing me."

"We?" she mumbled.

"Of course." I took out her compact and inspected my already-flawless makeup and bared my teeth to check for any imperfections.

I have to admit, I was a cosmetic surgery queen. If it could be worked on, I'd pretty much had it done. The only thing I'd failed to perfect was my derrière. An idea came to me.

"I'll show that black-hemian hoochie." I pulled out my cell phone and pressed 4 on the speed dial. "Hello, Marie. Catalina Richards speaking. I want to come in for a consultation for gluteus augmentation."

Sierra looked at me like I was crazy. Didn't she know about 24-hour cosmetic surgeons? I sighed and rolled my eyes.

I returned to my conversation. "Sure, Monday afternoon is fine. Great, see you then." I closed the phone and looked Sierra up and down, trying to figure out what demon had possessed her.

"I see someone has an attitude this time of the month," I snapped.

"It's *not* that time of the month. I just think you're starting to get a little batty. I mean, what happened so bad that it would cause you to go to these extreme measures? Seriously, Cat. Butt implants?"

"You just don't get it, do you? You don't understand what I have to lose."

"Of course. Lucas is a great guy and—"

I couldn't take it anymore. I had to tell someone. I couldn't hold onto my terrible secret in any longer.

"Forget that! We're broke, Sierra. You hear me? Broke."

She gave me a dumbfounded look. "We're broke?"

"Not you. Me. We. My family." I covered my face with my hands and began to sob.

"What? What the hell are you talking about?"

"They hate me," I sobbed.

She got off at the College Park exit and pulled into a parking lot."OK, now tell me what you're talking about."

The flood gates opened and I told Sierra all about what happened with my parents the day before.

* * *

My father called me Wednesday afternoon while I was at the nail salon seeing my nail tech Mikia, getting my permanent French manicure filled in.

"Catalina, darling, we need to talk."

"OK, Daddy, but what's this about? I'm at the nail salon right now and I won't be done until—"

"Come to the house when you're done with your appointment."

"OK." I closed my phone and put it backing my Fendi bag with the hand Mikia hadn't done yet.

On the way to my parents' house in Mitchellville, I went over a hundred things in my head about what he could want to talk to me about. I hoped it wasn't the get a job lecture or the do something productive seminar. Didn't he know what kind of effort it took to look the way I did?

I went to college at Spelman to appease my parents and got a degree in dance. I hadn't really used the degree up to that point, and I can't say I ever really thought about it. My goal was to marry money and do whatever I felt like every day, like many of my father's friends' wives.

My mother, Helena, was a beautiful woman who, even in her early fifties, had a body that could rival women half her age. She was a nice woman, but at times I thought she was too nice.

My father ran my grandfather's real estate development business, and he wasn't home much, so my mother talked him into buying her a dance studio to run. I would occasionally fill in to teach some of the classes, but kids got on my nerves, so I tried to limit that as much as possible. My father would get a tone with me when I refused to help out, but my mother would just sigh and go on about her business.

I pulled into the stately driveway and walked up the five

marble steps to my childhood home's front entrance. The place was sprawling. As a matter of fact, I could have easily taken one of the bedrooms in the far end of the house and probably would have never seen my parents, but instead I talked my father into leasing an luxury apartment for me in Dupont Circle.

My father opened the door and turned to walk back inside without saying a word. I huffed and closed the door before following him into the parlor, where my mother was sitting and sipping some hot tea.

"Hey, Mommy."

"Catalina." She slightly nodded and returned her attention to her tea.

My father motioned for me to take a seat in the white wingback chair across from the sofa while he took a seat next to my mother. I sat down and looked above their heads at the Bayo Iribhogbe painting. It was a scene of a crowd of people, all black white, and gray. In the center of the crowd was a red person, who stood out among the others. I was starting to feel like Mr. Red.

"Catalina, the reason we brought you here is that we need to have a serious discussion about your finances, or, lack thereof."

My heart dropped into my stomach. I was hoping it was going to be about something other than money. But it always came back to that.

"What about it, Daddy?" I looked at my mother, who refused to return my stare.

"Your mother and I feel it's time you start taking responsibility for yourself. You're older than Gina, yet she has already graduated with a Ph.D and owns her own home."

I rolled my eyes when they mentioned my younger sister,

Gina. She might have been responsible, but she let her appearance go and now resembled a fruit from the ugly tree.

"What we're trying to say is, we think it's time you grew up and took some initiative. We didn't send you to school to come home and live off of us."

I tried to speak, but my mother held up her finger.

"Catalina, we've given you seven years to figure something out, and we are out of time and patience. I tried to get you interested in my studio, and even tried to give you your own classes. But each time you disappointed me and your students by showing up late or not at all."

"Well, I can try again. I promise I'll try harder this time. Please, Mommy, just give me another chance." I gave my mother my sad eyes, but she wasn't fooled.

"I'm afraid you've run out of chances, dear."

My father cleared his throat and then picked up a file folder from the coffee table. He opened the folder, glanced at the contents, and then shook his head. He closed the folder and extended it to me.

"Catalina, there are $150,000 in plastic surgery bills in there. Now, I like to think I am an understanding and generous father, but this has gone too far."

I flipped through the various bills for my skin, breast, tummy, nose, and chin procedures, along with several other surgeries I had forgotten about.

"What do you want me to do, Daddy? Surely you don't expect me to pay for all of this."

My mother patted his hand and he said, "We want you to pay for half of it. And no more procedures."

"Well, how do you expect me to come up with $75,000?"

"I'm afraid that's your problem to deal with," my mother said.

I could feel my face getting hot and my temperature spike. I stood up from the chair and waved the folder in front of me. "Why are you doing this to me?"

"Darling, we want you to take responsibility for yourself. You are a grown thirty-year-old woman, yet everything you have is ours. Besides that, you have put us in a tight situation." She looked at my father for support. "And if we are forced to pay the $150,000, I will have to close my studio. We just won't be able to afford the expenses it takes to keep it running."

"We have to put a new roof on this house, which is going to cost an arm and a leg. We have our own expenses, and we just can't carry you all the time," my father said. "It's not fair to us or Gina that you do nothing and are given everything. It has to end now."

I stood there flabbergasted as my parents told their eldest, most beautiful daughter that they were about to cut her off.

"The money," I hiccupped. "It's almost gone. All of it. My parents hate me."

"How can it be gone? Is business not as good as it was for your father?"

"No, I said it's me. It's my fault. I did this to them, and now my mother might have to shut down her studio because they can't afford the rent. I have to fix it."

"OK, I get that part, even if you don't want to tell me what went down. But what does all this have to do with Lucas, Raquelle, and butt implants?"

"I can't lose him to her. He's my best chance to secure some money and get those bills paid and my parents off my back."

"I don't get it. How is marrying Lucas going to get you a

big chunk of change? I'm sure there will be a pre-nup agreement, and he won't go for you shelling out a bunch of his parents' cash to support your family."

"If I can get him to marry me, I'll be able to pay the bills." I took a deep breath and said nothing for the remainder of the ride home.

Chapter 7

Layla

The weekend had been uneventful after the Friday night catfight at Takoma Station. Hunter and I went to dinner and a movie Saturday and I came into the office to catch up on some paperwork Sunday. Monday was when all hell broke loose.

When I finally made it into the restroom and locked the door behind me that Monday morning, the face staring back at me strongly resembled a raccoon. I couldn't believe I had let my father make me break my cardinal rule: never cry at work.

The emergency board meeting had been called first thing that morning to address some major problems in the market that were, in turn, causing some major problems with some of our biggest clients. When I voiced my thoughts on what we could do to rectify the situation, my father just stared at me without saying a word. After the meeting adjourned, he came into my office and lit into me, telling me I was a disgrace to the firm for coming up with such hair-brained ideas. And I thought I was trying to think outside the box. Turns out I was being boxed in.

I surprised myself, though.

"Look, Mr. Lane. I demand the same respect you give to your other employees. In this firm, I am a senior associate, not your teenaged daughter. I don't appreciate you making me look like an ass in front of the board. If you can't extend that common courtesy to me, then I no longer wish to provide services for this firm."

"Then I suppose we won't be needing your services anymore. Thanks," he responded.

And with that, he left and slammed my door behind him so hard Lynette screamed. She looked at him, looked at me through the glass, and took off after him. What a puppy dog.

I pulled out one of my face towelettes and cleaned the mess off my face. As I wiped, I imagined the dirt I had put up with being erased from my memory.

Sometimes I thought my father wished Lucas was in my place at the firm and I was off being a trophy wife like my mother, Minerva. Oh, she had ties to several charitable organizations, but she still operated in Stepford wife mode most of the time. But I wanted a career, and Lucas had his own ideas about what he wanted from life, and working under my father at a finance firm wasn't one of them. I was finally starting to understand why. Lucas was making a difference in the lives of inner city children by teaching them music and giving them an outlet for the frustrations of coming up in the ghetto. I was just a glorified bean counter in a firm where I wasn't really wanted.

I left the building with only my pride and the few pictures

I had around my office, including me and Hunter at our engagement party and one of Raquelle and I at Essence Fest a few years back. I figured they could do whatever the hell they wanted with the rest of it.

When I got to the parking garage, there was a new guy in the ticket booth. He was also pretty handsome. He was light-skinned like Terrence Howard, but he had his hair cut low and he was a little thicker.

I walked over to him and said, "I have the navy blue Acura."

He grinned and turned to the pegboard that held the keys. "I know that car. I was just admiring it earlier. Very nice, Mrs.—"

"Miss Lane."

"Oh, like Lane & Associates?"

I paused. "No, like Lois."

It took him a moment, which gave me enough time to admire the bulges in his uniform. Biceps and more.

Finally he grinned and said, "Well, then just call me Clark." He winked and took off toward the second level, which gave me an alternate view; one that I liked just as much as the first.

He pulled my car up within a few moments. He stepped out and blocked my entrance. "So, Lois, can I have your card in case I need a sidekick?"

I had to smile. "I don't have one, but . . ."

He went over to the booth and came back with a small slip of scrap paper and a pen while I got in the driver's seat. I rolled down the window as he approached and wrote down my cell number. I felt guilty for doing it, but there was some kind of twinkle in his eyes that I couldn't say no to.

"Thanks, Lois."

"Anytime, Clark." I rolled up my window and left the garage with a mischievous smirk on my face.

I was feeling a little adrenaline rush after just doing two things that were totally out of character for me: standing up to my father and flirting with another man. A blue collar, fine one at that.

Hunter wasn't a bad guy. In fact, he was probably one of the most caring, responsible, stable people I knew. The thing that worried me with him, however, is the fact that there was no real spark between us. If someone told me they saw him with a female, I wouldn't get jealous. If I found a strange number on his cell phone, I wouldn't question him. If I came across a suspiciously sexy email, I wouldn't fly off the handle. That worried me, especially when I thought about the fact that I'd be spending the next fifty years with someone in complete indifference.

Hunter was from the same type of family I was from. My father, Jim Richards (Catalina's father), and Hunter's father all went to the same college, ran in the same circles, took all the right courses, made all the right contacts, and knew all the right people. Hunter went to medical school and now worked as a dermatologist in one of the most profitable facilities in the area. He worked alongside other dermatologists and plastic surgeons, catering to the most exclusive clients. Hunter had a good heart, though. He was just very easily swayed by what his parents thought was the right thing to do. Sometimes I think he and Catalina would have made a better match. Lucas and I were the veritable rebels of the group because we didn't take everything we were told at face value.

After leaving the office on my adrenaline high, I drove around for a little while, ate a Big Mac, and drove around some more. After realizing I had been driving for six hours, I went to Hunter's for some comfort and support. I was a little nervous that he would tell me I had acted rashly, but I was pleased by his reaction.

"I left Lane and Associates today."

"Of course you did. You're here with me, aren't you?" His eyes sparkled and his flawless skin gave off a glow.

"No I mean I *left* left. I quit. Got fired. Resigned." I recounted the day's events to him.

We were cuddling on his large sectional discussing what my next move should be. I was positioned between his legs, facing the television. He had his arms wrapped around my waist.

"I know you're upset, sweetie. But I don't think your father had malicious intent. Sometimes we don't realize the gravity of our words and actions until it's too late." He stroked my cheek.

"Yeah, I get what you're saying, but at the same time, it's just too much for me. I just can't handle working there anymore."

"Well, you have an impressive education and resume. I'm sure if you wanted to, you could secure a job at any of the big five firms."

"Yeah." I turned around to face him and began planting soft kisses on his lips. I was in the mood for a stress release, but, truth be told, I was thinking about my run-in with Clark Kent earlier, and it was making me pretty hot. I wasn't really sexually adventurous, but something came over me when he kissed me back passionately and rubbed the sides of my waist. I slid out of my skirt and turned around so he'd have a good view of my behind. I'm not saying I was into ass worship, but it turned me on when my curves were appreciated.

He ran his finger down the center of my cocoa-brown thong and planted a few kissed on each cheek. Since I wasn't looking at him, I was imagining the guy from the garage admiring my backside and sprinkling it with kisses.

I didn't turn around. I told him to lose his pants. Once I saw them in a pile next to my feet, I removed my shirt and bra and straddled his legs. He started to speak, but before he could form the words, I cut him off.

"Just let me lead, baby."

In a reverse cowgirl position, I grabbed his dick and lowered my wetness onto it. A rush of air escaped his lips and I closed my eyes and went to work, bobbing up and down. After a few seconds of the backwards ride, I found a good rhythm, and I could feel myself nearing my peak.

All of a sudden, he grabbed my waist and lifted me off of him. He flipped me over on my back and started going at me missionary style with my leg propped up on the back of the couch.

I was pissed for a couple reasons. First of all, when a woman is closing in on her climax, it's rude to interrupt. Secondly, I had tried to take the lead for once and do something different and rock his world and he basically dissed me.

I just laid there with fake oohs and ahhs coming out of my mouth until he finally blew his load and then jumped up to get in the shower.

Later, we lay in his bed. He was lightly snoring and I was heavily irritated. It wasn't that Hunter wasn't a good guy, I just knew at that moment that he wasn't the guy for me. I sneaked out of bed and grabbed my clothing, purse, and work bag from the armchair. I tiptoed into the master bath, sat on the toilet and retrieved a notepad and pen from my bag. Then I started writing.

Hunter,

Please understand that what I'm about to say has nothing to do with you and everything to do with me. I appreciate the love and kindness you have shown me over the past two years. You are a good man and any woman would be proud to have you. However, I am just not ready for marriage. I feel like there is something missing between us, and I can't move forward with this engagement with doubts lingering in my mind.

I don't expect you to wait for me to grow up, find myself, or anything like that. I want you to find someone who deserves the love you have to offer.

Love,
Layla
P.S. I am leaving the ring because I wouldn't feel right keeping it.

I placed the letter and the $55,000 Tiffany ring where I knew Hunter would find it first thing in the morning: on the bathroom sink, and quietly let myself out. When I closed my car door, the tears came. I think they were for a combination of the two years I had spent wondering if I was doing the right thing, the six years I had spent at my father's firm, and for the broken heart I knew Hunter would have when he read it. Despite the fact that the clock on my dashboard told me it was 1:00 A.M., I headed over to Raquelle's for some girl-friend support. I had just defied the person I had been for my entire life, and I knew if anyone knew defiance, it was my girl.

Chapter 8

Lucas
Monday

Sometimes you come across people you know are going to be great one day if they can just pull themselves out of the mess they were born into.

Jay-Ron was one of those people. He was one of my students at the public junior high I taught music at in Southeast. When I tell you the kid gave John Legend a run for his money, believe that. I had been teaching him piano for the last two years, and he picked it up like second nature. His talent wasn't what worried me, though. I was starting to worry that Jay-Ron was going to get caught up in some mess he had no business in. When he didn't show up for school for the second week straight, I knew something was off. So I decided to roll down to the hood and see what I could see.

I was born into privilege, and let me tell you, it can be a blessing and a curse. I guess I really didn't realize how different I was from the kids I was teaching until I went looking for Jay-Ron.

I had never seen The Green Bay Housing Project in real life. I'd seen plenty of news stories and photos, but seeing it in person was completely different. It was dusk when I crossed the Anacostia bridge, and I was starting to have second thoughts about rolling through the hood in an S-Type after dark, but something inside me told me I had to go.

I drove around the surrounding blocks a few times, making sure not to go too fast for fear of running someone over, but also not too slow, for fear the folks hanging outside would think I was either an easy car-jacking target or someone getting ready to do a drive-by.

After seeing no signs of Jay-Ron, I pulled up to the curb next to a carry-out and got out. I made sure to click the alarm, and a few of the brothers standing on the corner watched me and laughed. I wondered if they were laughing at me because I seemed so square or because I was about to be jacked.

I walked up to this thick guy wearing a black hoodie, jeans, a stocking cap, and some black Timbs.

"Excuse me, my brother. Do you know a kid by the name of Jay-Ron?"

He looked me up and down, from my neatly formed locks to my brown dress boots. "Who wants to know?"

"Oh, I'm his music teacher and I was getting worried when he didn't show up for a couple of weeks." I tried to harden my stance, but the brother just raised his eyebrow.

"His teacher, huh? Seems to me you in the wrong side of DC, man. Why don't you just take your ass back over to Georgetown and let us take care of our own?"

I raised my hands. "I don't want any trouble. I'm just worried about him."

About that time, a skinny, light-skinned kid, who looked

to be about Jay-Ron's age exited the carry-out with a white Styrofoam container.

He pointed to me with a white plastic fork and then turned to the brother I was speaking with. "Ay, Em, who dis fool?" he asked the man. He looked at my shoes and then turned his attention to my car. "Is this bamma lost or sumthin'?"

The man I deduced to be named Em never took his eyes off me. "Nah, he lookin' for Jay."

I noted that he used a shortened nickname for Jay-Ron, telling me he knew him.

"Oh. Why you looking for him? You looking for some blow?" the kid asked.

"NO. I was just worried when he didn't show up for school and—"

"What, you his daddy or su-in?" Em and the young kid started laughing, and I was embarrassed.

"Mr. Lane?"

I heard the voice over my shoulder. Em and the kid stopped laughing and focused behind me. I turned around and saw Jay-Ron dressed nearly identically to Em.

"Jay-Ron! I was looking for you. I got worried when—"

Jay-Ron held up his hand and said, "C'mon, Mr. Lane. Let's go for a ride." He gestured to my car.

We drove around for a while in silence until he broke it by asking, "Mr. Lane, why'd you come out here?" He scanned the streets.

"I just wanted to make sure you were okay. I was worried when you didn't come to class for so long. Where have you been?"

He looked down at his lap and then readjusted his stocking cap. "I been around. Just trying to survive." He rubbed the tan leather on his seat. "But I know you don't know nothing about that."

I felt a little insulted at first, but then I realized he was right. "Yeah, I guess."

He grunted.

"Seriously, Little Man, I think you can really go places with your talent. If I had as much raw talent that you have in your little finger, I'd be on top of the world."

"Yeah, well, talent don't mean a lot out here. It's more about what you gonna eat that day, or IF you gonna eat."

"Well, let me help you out. I'll take you to the store and we can pick up some things."

"Nah. You take me to make groceries, I'll get used to it, and we both know I can't afford that." He rubbed his chin and looked at me as I stopped at a stop sign.

"Well, I can help you again. Where is your mother? Why is she letting you skip school?"

"My mama died last year. It's just been me and my sister. Nikki ain't 'bout nothing, though. All she cares about is being bunned up under Ace."

"I'm sorry, Jay-Ron. I had no idea—"

"You ain't got nothing to be sorry about. You ain't kill her. 'Less your name is breast cancer." He looked out the window and I just sat there a minute before a white Excursion honked at me for sitting at the stop sign too long.

"Ahh, shit. That's Ace." Jay-Ron slumped down in his seat.

"Who's Ace? Your sister's boyfriend?"

"Nobody."

I drove to the Safeway I'd passed on my way in and parked near the door. "Come on."

Jay-Ron remained slumped in his seat but peeked up long enough to scope out the lot. "I'm straight."

"All right, man, but don't be mad when I come out with Grape Nuts and organic goat cheese for you to take home." I kept my face completely solemn.

"Ahh, man." He unbuckled his seat belt and we both went into the store.

We filled up an entire buggy full of frozen meals, cereal, canned foods, and sandwich fixings. The total was close to two hundred and fifty dollars, but to me, it was well worth it.

Jay-Ron directed me to his apartment building, and we loaded the plastic bags into my portable cart. When we stepped into the elevator, I thought I would gag from the piss smell.

He looked embarrassed enough, so I didn't say anything. When we stepped out onto the sixth floor, there was a large man with a white bandana and matching velour sweatsuit staring at us.

Jay-Ron just gave him a nod and we proceeded to his apartment. We stepped inside, and I have to admit, I was surprised by the cleanliness of the place. It stood in stark contrast to the exterior and elevator. I unloaded the bags for him and moved toward the kitchen when he stepped in front of me.

"Look, Mr. Lane. I really appreciate this, but I think it's best I walk you out now."

I was confused, but nodded and followed him back outside. There were two females and the man in white leaning against my Jag.

"Ay, get the fuck off his car," Jay-Ron yelled.

I looked at Jay-Ron in shock. I'd never heard him curse before. What surprised me more was the fact that the large man and the girls quickly obliged, mumbling their apologies.

"Thanks again," he said after turning to me.

"No problem. I expect to see you in class Thursday."

"Bet."

As I pulled off, I couldn't help but look back in my rearview mirror. I saw Jay-Ron extract something from his pocket. About six or seven scruffy-looking men and a couple of women approached him, each waiting their turns for whatever he was giving out.

I spoke to Catalina later that night. I was surprised to hear from her because she'd been basically MIA since the club incident. I made the mistake of thinking I could confide in my fiancée and told her about the experience of going to see Jay-Ron.

"You know, Lucas, when you lie with dogs, you might catch fleas."

"What the fuck did you just say?" I could feel the heat rising to my face.

"I'm just saying, we aren't like those people you teach. We come from a different pedigree, a different world. I guess now you finally realized that. Why don't you see if your father can get you in the doors at Sidwell F—"

"What are we, dogs? What makes you think I *want* to change jobs? Why do you think I would prefer to teach snotty, privileged kids instead of kids who don't have a fighting chance to—"

"That's just it, baby. They don't have a fighting chance. So why waste your time? They'll probably end up being drug dealers or welfare mothers anyway."

My forefinger involuntarily pressed the END button on the cordless.

Whoops.

She tried to call back for the next hour, but I set the base to DO NOT DISTURB. I guessed there was a chance she'd show up at the house if she couldn't get through via phone, but I dismissed the thought after remembering it was her weekly facial night, and she probably wouldn't leave her home.

After the boy-not-from-the-hood experience and listening to Catalina talk that snobbish pedigree nonsense, I realized I had actually never researched my family and my pedigree. I knew my mother was a debutante back in the day, and her parents had some kind of travel business and a summer home in Martha's Vineyard, but I never knew much about my father's family. It was almost like he was an island. I didn't have any aunts, uncles, cousins, or grandparents I could remember.

I went to ancestry.com and started building my family tree. I searched all the names on my mother's side of the family I could remember and had a nice list built up.

When I went to do my father's branches it got much more difficult. I typed in his full name, but all the search returned were some records for a guy with the same name having been born in Southeast D.C. and married in 1974 to a woman I had never heard of. I knew that couldn't be my pop. Plus, there was no record of this Kelvin Frederick Lane marrying my mother, Minerva Randall. It seemed like a stretch that there would be two men with the exact same name, but the info just didn't add up to be my father.

"Can't be him."

I sighed and saved my work before logging out of the site. I'd have to do a little more research before I'd be able to complete my family tree. I was frustrated, and my eyes were getting tired and I had an early morning ahead of me so I shut down my computer and headed to bed. As I lay there, I couldn't help fantasizing about Raquelle in that skirt until I drifted off.

Chapter 9

Raquelle

Evan never had a problem pleasing me in the bedroom. I think, in a lot of ways, that was why I kept him around so long. I remember some pretty nasty freak sessions with my boy. He always made sure I came before him, even if he had to hold out while pounding me doggy-style while I fondled my clit. As a matter of fact, I had only had one orgasm with a man during straight-up intercourse, and you guessed it, it was with Evan. I was mad turned on because we had been watching some pretty steamy porn, but nevertheless, I came without any direct clitoral stimulation. Just thinking about that episode made me squirm on my way home from work. When I got in the house, I had to get Purple Lucas out to calm my ass down.

I was torn about the meeting with Evan. Part of me wanted to run off to Siberia and pretend I'd never agreed to it, and another part of me wanted to hear him out. Plus, I was feenin' like a mug for some of Paco's spaghetti and quesadillas. Paco's was a Mexican-Sicilian fusion place in Georgetown. I asked the staff once why there was such a wide variety of food. The waiter told me it was due to Paco's mixed heritage.

I slipped into my rust-colored hippie shirt, some Diesel jeans, and some brown Diesel pumps. I loved the way rust set off my complexion and the jeans accented my booty. I applied some simple bronze lipstick and sprayed just a touch of Magnetism on my neck and wrists before heading out the door.

When I got to the restaurant, I saw Evan sitting at the bar talking to the bartender. He looked muscular and handsome in his gold polo shirt and dark jeans. The place was fairly empty, but a few folks dressed in business attire were sprinkled throughout the dining area.

I walked up next to Evan. "Still drinking Killian's, I see."

He whipped his head around and the bartender gave me a wink before asking me if I would like anything.

"No, thanks. I'll just wait until we're seated." I smiled at him and turned back to Evan, who was slightly agape.

"You ready to eat?" I asked, ignoring his stare and the unwelcome heat that it caused to crawl up my neck.

"Sure." He stood and we moved to the hostess, who seated us at a booth near the window. I looked everywhere but at him—the menu, the red and white checks on the tablecloth, and even the votive burning in an understated glass holder.

"I can't believe this is happening. I've waited so long for this," he said.

I looked into his caramel-colored eyes, which seemed to instantly tear up, and knew he meant it.

"It's been a long time," I responded.

"Ay, I wanted to tell you I'm sorry for bustin' up in your job like that. That was messed up of me."

"Don't worry about it." I went back to poring over the

menu, although I had known I wanted spaghetti since I woke up that morning.

We sat through the meal in relative silence, with him pausing frequently to stare at me, particularly when I had a marinara-drenched spaghetti noodle dangling from my mouth. When I felt his eyes on me, my mind would go back to the freaky memories that we shared. A few times, my mind even went back to the romantic times, like when he would serenade me with Maxwell or Jaheim or I would come home and find him making grilled cheese for me.

The waiter brought the check and we both reached for it.

"I got this," he said. "I'm the one who asked you."

I shrugged. "OK."

After he paid and tipped nicely, we went outside.

"Wanna walk?" he asked.

I hesitated, then shrugged. "Why not?"

We walked up Wisconsin Avenue past the shops and restaurants. It was still light outside, but there was a slight chill in the air. Without warning, Evan grabbed my hand and held it in his as we continued up the street. I didn't protest. It actually felt kinda nice.

"Rocky, I want you back. I can't sleep without you." He smiled and then sang a little bit of R. Kelly's tearjerker. "I can't sleep, baby. I can't think, baby."

I couldn't help but crack a little grin. "You still remember that song?"

"Girl, all I had up in prison was time to remember." He stopped walking and looked me in the eyes. "I remembered how we loved each other, how we had each other's backs. I was tore up when you stopped writing and taking my calls."

I continued the walk. "I didn't know what to do. I was so pissed at you for doing stupid shit."

"I know. I was pissed at me too."

We turned around and started back toward Paco's after the street turned more residential. When we approached my car, something came out of my mouth that surprised even me.

"You wanna come over and continue this conversation?"

"Hell yeah!"

I gestured to my car. "This is me. Follow me."

He nodded and took off toward a red Cavalier.

On the ride home, I kept flashing back to the sexcapades and good lovin'. My panties were wet by the time I parked and waited for him to follow me up the steps. I took his hands in my face and kissed him. His lips were just as soft as I remembered, and his strong hands encircled my waist. I could feel his dick getting hard and pressing up against me. It was on.

We didn't even get in the door good before we were ripping each other's clothes off. I briefly held concern for my shirt, which had been worn only twice, but the thought faded when I felt how hard he was. I mean he was hard. Jailhouse-with-no-conjugal-visits-and-too-much-whacking-off hard.

I looked down at the piece of man-steel and pushed him back on the couch. As I was preparing to straddle him, I remembered a condom.

"Don't you fuckin' move." I ran into my bedroom and pulled all the clutter out of my nightstand drawer before I found my emergency stash of condoms. I ran back into the living room and he was standing up, dick at full attention.

"What are you doing? I told you not to move."

"I want to please you first, 'cause I can't say how long I'll be able to last."

It was like I just remembered he had been locked down

with a bunch of burly dudes for three years. I nodded my affirmation and walked over to put on the CD he gave me. Then I placed the condom on the end table and sat on the couch. I pulled his arm to bring him close to me.

I leaned back in what I call the X-rated couch stance. My butt was just at the edge of the seat cushions and my legs were up. He started kissing my inner thighs, caressing my feet, and softly touching my pussy.

"Mmm. Girl, you have no idea how many times I thought about this." He rubbed both sides of my lips gently before parting them and moving his face closer. I could feel his hot breath on me before his tongue took its first taste. He licked and held my leg with one hand while he slowly inserted a finger from his other hand.

Now, remember. I had been on sexual hiatus for a while. Granted, I had my share of toys, movies, and playing with myself, but trust me when I tell you, ain't *nothing* like the real thing. He was worried that he would come too fast, but he shouldn't have sweated it. Within two minutes, I was screaming and curled up into a little ball. He gave me a moment to collect myself, and then we got right back into our old groove and he gave me a nice thug pounding.

Afterward, we lay there silent for a good half hour. I would look over at him and he'd be staring at me. When I'd say, "What?" he'd just smile and say "Nothing."

Until . . .

"Rocky, I can't live without you. I understand I made some fucked up decisions, but I need you."

"Hmmm."

"I know I never told you what really went down, well, except for in those letters. But anyway, I want to get it all out there."

He proceeded to tell me how he was trying to help out his mother and treat me to the finer things. He said he got caught up in the fast money, and got used to the things he was able to do with it. I felt a little bad, but I wasn't going to take the blame for him selling drugs.

"I know you're not trying to put this on me or your mama."

"Nah, never that. I'm just letting you know what was going through my head. What I was trying to do. I meant well, but I just didn't know how much it would cost me. Especially if I had to lose you over it, never mind three years of spending time without you and my ma." He paused and a sad look came across his face. "She passed, you know."

"Wow. No, I didn't know. I'm so sorry. What happened?" I wrapped my arms around him and felt his breathing become a little jagged.

"She had brain cancer. Look, I know I fucked up. But I want to show you I changed."

I pulled back and looked into his eyes. "I'm willing to try. I think I understand things better now."

"See? If you woulda read my letters, you woulda understood three years ago." He moved out of my embrace, playfully punched my arm, and then leaned over to give me another one of those passionate kisses. We lay there for hours, catching up, chatting, being silent. Kissing. Making love. Straight fucking. And beginning the cycle all over again.

After another strenuous round, I went to the bathroom and saw that it was close to midnight. I knew I had to be at work at seven, so I was getting tired just thinking about it. I wrapped myself in my orange, fuzzy robe and went back to Evan.

"It's getting late." I yawned. "And I have an early morning."

"Oh, ok. That's cool. Let's go to bed then."

"Evan, look. I'm not there just yet. I need some time to process what just went down."

"Ok, I can respect that." He went to the bathroom and came back a few minutes later, fully dressed with his keys in his hand.

"You don't know how happy this makes me." He grinned.

"I think we're gonna be okay this time around." I hugged him and walked him to the door.

I kissed him good-night and went and jumped in the shower. I sang as loud as I could while the mango-scented suds cascaded over my body. I was feeling giddy from the multiple orgasms, but there was still something bothering me. Now, I know I told you I was searching for that "can't be without cha, baby" kind of love, but I wondered if Evan was the one who could truly give me that. Sex was great, but sex with someone you are in crazy love with is ten times better.

When I turned the water off, I heard a banging noise. My stomach did a little flip as I wrapped the bath sheet around me and went to the door. I looked out the peephole and saw Layla standing on my stoop.

"Girl, you almost scared me to death. I was in the shower and heard a loud-ass noise. I was having some *Psycho* visions."

"Sorry. I just need to talk."

She walked past me and sat on the couch. I cringed, thinking what had just taken place in that very spot less than an hour before.

"Be right back." I went and changed into some pajamas and then made us a cup of hot chocolate. I handed her a mug and sat down in my brown leather recliner.

"So, what's the malfunction?"

She went on to tell me what all had gone down that day,

ending the crazy story with her writing a Dear John letter to Hunter.

I was a little thrown off by it all. I guess it shouldn't have been a surprise that she was unhappy with Hunter, but I was surprised she finally took a stand for herself.

"I just need a change. I feel like I've been stuck in a rut— no, a canyon for the last five years."

"I feel you. Sometimes it's hard for me to get up in the morning knowing I have to do the same thing I do every day. And I'm about through with those dirty old men who come in and use the labs."

She nodded. "Going through the motions. Let me ask you this, then, since I have no idea of what my answer is. If you could step out on faith and do anything, what would you want to do?"

"Are we having an Oprah moment?" I laughed and then got serious. "Wow. The truth? I would love to use my Human Sexuality degree. Maybe open up a practice."

"Your WHAT?"

"Yeah, girl. I've been keeping it a secret for the last few years, but I've been taking night and online classes for Human Sexuality. I got my master's."

Her mouth dropped open and she leaned forward. "What the hell? Are you serious? Why did you hide it? When . . . ? Wow."

"I don't know. I guess I thought people would think I was crazy or silly or I don't know. It's just been a passion for a long time. I like learning about sex and passing on my knowledge. Now, putting it into practice has been a little problematic the last year or so with my hiatus, but I think that's going to change."

Layla raised her eyebrow and then leaned back. She took

off her black Guess driving glasses and placed them on the end table—right beside the condom wrappers. I sat there and prayed she didn't look too hard.

"So what kind of practice would you open? I've gotta hear this."

"A place where people could feel comfortable and open about learning how to make their sex lives better. I'd have classes for different subjects, ya know, Pussy Eating 101." I laughed and then imagined the other courses I could offer.

She paused for a moment. "Well, let's do it then."

"Do what?" I looked at her like she had lost her mind.

"Open the practice. A freak school."

"Freak school? Hmmm, I like that." My heart was racing, but then reality struck me. "I'd need a lot of start up money, though. And Lord knows I don't have much of that."

"Let me worry about that."

"What? But you just quit your job and—"

"Heffa, I have more than enough stashed away. I didn't go to finance school for nothing."

The excitement returned. "Ahhh, shit. It is going to be on."

I could tell the wheels were turning inside her head. "What would we call it?"

I searched the nooks, crannies, and crevices of my brain. "Hmmm, Rocky's Whore Picture Show?"

We busted out laughing. Once we calmed down a little, I said, "Rocky's Rock Hard Pussy Palace?"

"Oh hell no. That sounds like a brothel," she screamed.

I couldn't help but giggle. "Ok, ok. Well, let me think about what I would want to accomplish. Ok. Teaching men how to please their women. Learning about toys and techniques.

Teaching women how to be a lady in the streets and a freak in the sheets."

"That's it." Layla jumped up out of her seat and screamed. "What?"

"Freak in the Sheets!"

I mulled it over for a second before doing my Lil Jon impression. "Yeea-yah."

We were up the entire night making notes, coming up with a plan, and eating Velveeta Shells and Cheese. When 5:30 hit and it was time for me to get ready for work, Layla gathered her notes and went to grab her glasses off the table.

"Umm, Raquelle? What are those?" She pointed to the six bright red condom wrappers.

"Oh, those? I was, umm, testing their durability. Yeah, I was running some experiments." I nodded.

"Uh-uh. I know you better than that. Who, might I ask, was the guinea pig?"

I mumbled, "Evan." Then I ran into the bathroom and slammed the door.

"Evan? What? When? Oh my God. You hussy!"

She opened the bathroom door and said, "Explain, please."

I had forgotten to lock the damn thing. I sighed. "Ok, damn. He was here. We went to dinner. We came back here. We had sex. We talked. We're back together." I chose that moment to shove my electric toothbrush into my mouth.

"Well, well, well. See how it is? I break up and you kiss and make up." She laughed. "Why the sudden change of heart? I thought you were done with him."

I just smiled with a little white foam escaping out of the corner of my mouth.

"And I thought you were in love with my dear little brother."

I spit. "Well, I can't wait forever for him to wake up and kick that snobby bitch to the curb." I continued brushing.

"You're right. He's a mess. Add Catalina to the mix and you have a hot mess. Shoot, even more of a mess than me and Hunter were."

I just nodded and spit.

Chapter 10

Lucas

I agreed to see Catalina about two weeks after our fight. I didn't call her back for about a week after I hung up on her after the Jay-Ron thing, which still hadn't been resolved. He showed up that Thursday for his lesson, but I hadn't seen him since, and I was wondering about that guy Ace who seemed to shake him up.

I was burning some candles and playing Leela James and "When You Love Somebody" came on. I couldn't help but think about Raquelle. She had that soul sista vibe going on like Leela. I figured Raquelle probably had the CD.

My thoughts were interrupted by my downstairs buzzer. Catalina's voice came across the speaker, "Hey baby. It's me."

I buzzed her up and turned the stereo down. She hated Leela James. Said she dressed like a homeless person and her hair looked like she hadn't washed it in months. What that had to do with her singing skills, I had no clue. Anyway, I thought Leela was kinda cute.

When Catalina walked through the door, my first thought

was, *Did she grow an ass in a week?* Followed by, *What the hell has she been eating?* Whatever the case, I had to admit she looked good. She was wearing a baby blue tank with little sparkly things on it and some tight jeans that had me thinking some seriously impure thoughts. Her hair was wavy and hung down below her shoulders, and her makeup was understated. I even thought I smelled the slight essence of coconut drifting from her form. I was a little surprised because I had never smelled anything but Chanel coming from her, and I had never seen her hair less than bone-straight.

"Why are you looking at me like that?" She smiled and ran her hand over her waves.

"You look . . . different."

"You like?"

"Yeah, it's nice." I reached over and touched her hair and then twirled her around. "What've you been eating? Chicken and dumplings? Biscuits and gravy?"

She giggled. "Don't you worry about that. Just know that it's all for you."

I wondered when the aliens that had kidnapped the real Catalina and replaced her with this stand-in were going to make the switch back. She carried a paper bag into the kitchen and extracted some Italian takeout boxes. She looked in all my cabinets until she found my plates. None of them matched, but she didn't seem to care. She came into the living room, handed me a plate, and sat hers down on the coffee table. She paused for a moment, moving her head toward the stereo speakers.

"Is that Lilah Jones?"

I laughed under my breath. "Uhh, Leela James."

"Right. Well, can we turn it up?"

I was a little stunned, and it took me a moment to form a

response. "Uhhm sure." I hit the volume button a couple of times on the remote and turned my attention to the chicken parmigiana that sat before me. Catalina returned with a bottle of red wine and silverware.

"I have glasses," I reminded her.

"I know, but I thought it would be romantic to drink it out of the bottle."

I raised an eyebrow, but decided to dig into the dinner instead of trying to analyze what the alien was doing.

After we ate, and the wine had considerably kicked in, Catalina shocked me by getting up and swaying her new hips to the music. She started undressing slowly and soon I found my fly open, my dick out, and Catalina's mouth around it. She wasn't really doing anything fancy, but I was happy for whatever I was getting. Like I said before, we were pretty much limited to missionary.

She actually bent over and asked me to do it doggy style, and I was turned on by the new look of her from behind. The only problem was, when I closed my eyes, I saw Raquelle looking back at me over her shoulder.

After the sex, we lounged on the sofa and listened to the next CD in the changer, which happened to be an old Aretha compilation. Then, the aliens took back their decoy and brought back Catalina.

"I was thinking, we should set a date."

"Sure. Let's go to the movies Friday night."

"No, silly." She giggled. "I mean a date for our wedding."

"Come on, Cat. Let's not ruin this moment."

The fire returned to her eyes and her silicone breasts bobbed up and down as she yelled. "What do you mean ruin? I thought I was doing what you wanted. I thought I was being who you wanted."

"What are you talking about?"

The mood had successfully been destroyed, so I got up and found my jeans and put them back on.

"All of this." She stood and smacked her backside and then grabbed the ends of her hair.

"There's more to it than that."

"What else is there to it?" She got dressed and picked up the wine bottle. She turned it up and disappointed that it was empty, slammed it down on my marble coffee table.

"What the hell is wrong with you?"

She had a crazy look in her eyes. "I want you to set a date. Tonight. Or it's over."

I wasn't going to be punked. Not this time. "Ok, then. It's over. You can see yourself out." I threw on my T-shirt and went into the bathroom and closed the door and locked it.

I stared at myself in the mirror while I heard her out in the living room crying. Shortly thereafter, I heard some glass break and a large crash. Then I heard nothing. Fearing the worst, I slowly opened the bathroom door and looked out to see the room empty. The wine bottle had been shattered, my stereo was on the floor, and the door was wide open.

At first I got mad, but then I just closed the door to the apartment and sat down. I started asking myself why I couldn't fully commit to Catalina. After all, we were engaged. The only thing left to do was walk down the aisle. Then, it hit me. The nagging voice returned, and this time I could hear it plain as day.

"I don't love her."

Chapter 11

Layla

I was sitting outside drawing up our business plan with Raquelle at a café in Dupont Circle when a snooty, light-skinned lady walked out of a nearby salon and brutally reminded me of my mother. The woman was impeccably adorned in designer duds. Not the kind where the logo is plastered all over the front of the clothing; the kind that you had to have a nose for fashion to even recognize.

My mother never was the most gentle or loving person on the planet; at least not for as long as I've known her. She was the type of woman who would tell you to go fix your own boo-boo if you wrecked your bike. She never listened throughout the year so she could get you the perfect, meaningful gift on your birthday. And for as long as I can remember, she never said a lovey-dovey word to my father. Nor had I ever seen them embrace or kiss passionately.

Part of me thought this was why I thought it was normal for there to be no spark in a relationship. However, as I got older, I came to know there was more to love than last names and addresses.

I was scared for myself, but I was a more scared for Lucas. When I look at Catalina, I see my mother in a lot of ways. That's probably why my mother worshiped the ground Catalina walked on. They're both so engrossed in themselves, they see nothing else around them. I can attest that that's no place for a child to grow up. Never mind the fact that Catalina was a psycho. The Takoma Station scene replayed in my head.

"Earth to Layla!"

"Sorry. What were you saying?"

"I was telling you that our license was approved. All I had to do was prove my education and present the business plan, and they granted it to us."

"Great! Now all we have to do is find a space. We can hook it up with our decorating skills, but it has to be a special space." I flipped through the real estate section of the *Times*. For the past two weeks, Raquelle and I had been doing research on sex education schools. We found most of them were uptight and stuffy. We wanted Freak in the Sheets to be hipper, fresher, and more exciting. We both agreed that the key to all that was first finding the perfect space for the school.

Raquelle adjusted the collar on her black blazer. "Exactly. I don't want it to seem staunch or uptight. I think we need to make it warm, comfortable, but sexy and funky."

"Agreed."

My cell phone rang and I saw Hunter's number flash across the caller ID. I let it go to voicemail and returned my attention to the paper. This was only the ten thousandth time he had called since I had left him the letter two weeks before. It seemed like two years ago, and I was enjoying my freedom. Some of his messages started to sound pretty disturbing and desperate, so I just deleted them without listening.

We ordered some salads and sandwiches as we continued to peruse the paper and write down promotional and décor ideas. As the waitress was leaving our table after dropping off our check, my cell phone rang again. I seriously considered dropping it into my glass of water until I noticed it wasn't Hunter this time.

"Lucas? What's going on, little brother?"

"Just on my way to the other school. I hadn't talked to you for a while, so I thought I'd see what you're up to. Mother called me and told me you quit the firm and poor Hunter. So what are you doing with yourself?"

"Raquelle and I are exploring a . . . business venture."

"Oh, really? What kind of business?"

"We want to keep it quiet for now. You know, we don't want to jinx ourselves."

"Mmm. Okay then."

"So what have you been up to? How's your fiancée?"

"I don't have one."

"What?"

"I broke it off with her last night. She has too many problems. She had a damn butt augmentation thinking it was going to get me to set a wedding date."

I couldn't control my laughter. Raquelle looked up from her notes with a raised eyebrow and curious grin. I held up my index finger.

"She's a piece of work. But, seriously, I'm happy for you."

"Same here. I realized I didn't love her and no amount of time, or booty, was going to change that."

"I hear you."

"I'm happy for you too. I hope you're following your heart for once instead of always following your head."

"I love you."

"Love you too, sis. Look, I just pulled up to the school. I've gotta run."

"Ok, have a good day."

"You too. And tell Raquelle I said hello."

I smiled. "Will do."

After I ended the call, I looked up to find Raquelle still looking at me, waiting for an explanation. When I told her what he said, a look of joy, then sadness, then frustration came across her face.

"What?" I asked. "Are you having a *Sybil* moment?"

She laughed at my reference to our favorite movie when we were in high school. "No. I couldn't be happier that he got rid of that lunchbox."

"Ok, so why do you look like someone just kicked your puppy?"

"It's nothing. Oh hell. It just seems like every time there's an opening with me or Lucas, the other one is hopelessly unavailable."

"It's that deep?" I knew she had a crush on Lucas, but I never thought it was anything more than simple infatuation.

"Nah, not that deep." She sighed.

I knew that was a lie.

"Tell the truth, you hoochie."

"Not right now, woman. I want to focus on the task at hand."

I shrugged. "So, let's go look at these places." I lifted the newspaper and pointed to the properties I'd circled.

She nodded, I dropped a twenty on the table, and we left.

* * *

Later that night, Raquelle and I were cooking dinner at her house and celebrating the space we leased in the trendy Adams Morgan area. To the naked eye, it looked like it needed a lot of work, but to us, it was perfect. We had already gone to Home Depot and Ikea to look at some paint swatches and get some ideas. We had decided that each classroom would be painted a different color, each one lending its own brand of sensuality to the atmosphere.

I was sitting at her kitchen table while she whipped up a batch of jambalaya.

"We need margaritas," I said.

She pointed to her drink mixer on the counter and said, "Hook it up."

As I mixed our drinks, adding some Grand Marnier and Patrón Silver to the mixture of lime juice and a splash of lemonade, I started thinking about Lucas.

"So are you going to tell me the truth about what you were thinking when I told you about Lucas and Catalina?"

She stopped slicing the andouille sausage she had just cooked. She shrugged and resumed the slicing. "You know how I feel. Lucas needed to get away from her."

"Yeah, but something tells me it's deeper than that. Hey, I know you've always had a thing for him."

"Yeah, but I'm kinda caught up with Evan right now."

"Oh."

"Yeah. I already feel bad enough about not giving him a chance to explain himself when he got locked up. I couldn't just dump him after all that." She took the glass I was extending to her. "Plus, Lucas is dealing with a breakup. I wouldn't want to try to get with him and be the rebound chick."

"Please." I took a sip of my drink. "He hasn't really been

with Catalina for a long time. It's like I said, going through
the motions. Just like I was doing."

"Yeah, but still."

"Ok, I'm going to leave it alone."

I could hear my cell phone ringing in my purse in the living room, and since I had designated a special ringer for
Hunter, I knew it wasn't him. I ran in to grab it, and looked
at the caller ID. It was a Maryland number I didn't recognize.

"Hello?"

"May I speak to Ms. Lane, please?"

"Speaking. May I ask who's calling?"

"Jabar."

"Jabar?" I scanned my memory bank and came up empty.

"Oh, um, Clark Kent."

I lowered the phone and made a silent screaming motion.
"Oh, hey. I didn't think you were going to call."

"My fault. I meant to call earlier, but I got busy with some
things."

"Oh, I see. Listen, I'm over at a friend's house having dinner, but can I call you back later?"

"Oh, yeah. No problem. I'll be waiting by the phone,
Lois."

I grinned and said, "Ok, then. I'll talk to you then."

I didn't notice Raquelle come up behind me, so I jumped
a little when she said, "What was that all about? Who has you
grinning like a fifty-year-old woman who just had her first orgasm?"

"You and those metaphors. It was a guy I met."

"A guy?" She poked me in the side.

"Yes, a guy. But I'm not getting wrapped up in it. We have
too much work to do for me to get distracted."

"I heard that. Well, come on, let's eat."

Over dinner, we discussed some promotional ideas and brainstormed on how to get people to sign up for the classes. We decided on a website where people could read course descriptions and register for classes as well as placing postcards in salons, spas, and erotic toy stores around the area.

After we cleaned up, we were both tired, and truthfully, I wanted to get home to call my super man.

Chapter 12

Catalina

For two weeks after Lucas officially broke it off with me, I stayed in my apartment and didn't answer or make any phone calls, except to deliver food every other day. I felt like the walls were closing in on me, so I decided to go see my only real friend.

When Sierra pulled up to her townhouse, I was sitting on the front steps looking a crying mess and mumbling to myself. She approached me slowly, looking afraid that this would be a hostile situation.

"Cat?"

". . . and this can't be happening. I don't know what else to do because I thought I did what he wanted and I thought I was doing the right thing, but I did that and it didn't work and he doesn't want me and—"

"Whoa, slow down. What are you talking about?"

I jumped up and she flinched a little, but I hugged her instead of attacking her. My arms were around her neck, and I was nearly hanging my one hundred and twenty pound frame on her.

"Stop that. You're going to make me—"

She couldn't hold me any longer, and we both fell backward onto her wet, freshly-sodded, newly sprinkled lawn. It knocked the wind out of her, and she just laid there until she could catch her breath. My arms were still around her neck, and a lady who passed by walking her dog looked over at us, gasped, and quickly turned away before saying, "Come on, Tippy," to her little Cocker Spaniel.

"Catalina, you're going to have to get off me."

I lifted my head off the ground.

"Shit!" Sierra pushed me off her and inspected her ivory blazer.

"Come on," she said as she offered me her hand. "Let's go inside and talk about this."

I sniffled, wiped my nose and then grabbed her hand. She dug in her purse, found her keys, and unlocked the door. She motioned for me to go in first. I ran into the bathroom down the hall and slammed the door closed. Then came the shrill wails.

I heard her tapping on the bathroom door. "Cat, come out of there."

"I can't. My life is ooooooverr," I cried.

"I can't help you unless you come out of there and tell me what's going on."

It was funny how the tables had turned in our relationship. Suddenly, she was the one in control, and I was looking for her help.

After another five minutes of her pleading with me, I finally came out and followed her into the living room, taking my usual place on the chaise.

"Ok, tell me what happened."

"He called it off." I sniffed.

"Lucas? Why?"

"I asked him to set a date and he called it off."

She gave me a confused look, so I told her what happened when I went to his apartment with my look and new booty.

"I don't know what I'm going to do now. My father told me the plastic surgery bills have wiped him out. He told me I need to start working so I can pay them off and he can keep mom's studio open. I'm just not cut out for it, Sierra. I'm just not." I crossed my arms and leaned back.

"Why did you even go to college, Catalina? Why didn't you just get knocked up right out of high school by some rich man?"

"That would have been ideal, but my father told me I wouldn't get an allowance unless I completed school. Now, my parents told me they need the money now, and they won't even give me my allowance. What am I gonna do?"

She just stared at me for a minute then shook her head. "Well, it looks like you had better start looking for a job," she told me.

I shot daggers her way. "I don't know why I expected you to understand. You're practically blue-collar."

"Ok, you just crossed the line. I think you need to leave before I say something I will regret."

I huffed and flipped my hair before leaving. I didn't even bother to slam the door for effect.

I decided to straighten myself up and find a way to get what I wanted. I didn't even care anymore if it was Lucas or some other rich bastard. I just knew I had let myself slip and

I needed to get back up before I completely fell off the deep end.

I decided to go shopping and see my stylist to get myself together on the outside. I wasn't going to find a rich man looking like I did.

I saw the glossy postcard-sized flyer for Freak in the Sheets Pleasure Institute when I was waiting to get my hair done at Makeba's salon. There was a photo of a woman in a blue corset and short skirt. She had on glasses and gave off that sexy librarian or secretary vibe. She was standing over a man who was seated in a chair and blindfolded. The text under the picture said: SET YOUR LOVE LIFE FREE. EXPERIENCE AND GIVE PLEASURE BEYOND YOUR WILDEST IMAGINATION. BI, STRAIGHT, GAY, CURIOUS, MALES, FEMALES, ALL WELCOME. VISIT FREAKINTHESHEETS. COM FOR CLASS SCHEDULES AND DESCRIPTIONS. GRAND OPENING PARTY SATURDAY NIGHT. FOR MORE INFORMATION, CONTACT ROCKY AT 202-555-8989 OR VISIT US ONLINE AT FREAKINTHESHEETS.COM.

My heart skipped a beat. Rocky? That man-stealing bitch was starting a sex school? I started formulating a plan in my head.

"What'cha got there?" Makeba's voice brought me out of the trance I was in. She was eating some disgusting cheese popcorn.

"Looks like a flyer. I saw it sitting here." I tossed the flyer back onto the coffee table with the hair books and stood. "Are we ready?"

"Umph." She tilted the snack-sized bag up to her mouth to get the remaining crumbs out. "Freak in the Sheets. Lawd, girl. People will try to sell anything these days." She picked up the card and threw it into a trashcan on our way back to her chair.

She got me back to looking like my old self. My press and

curl was flawless, and she had shaped my brows and applied some make-up. I admired myself for a few minutes in her mirror before I remembered what I had seen earlier.

When I was leaving the salon, I casually returned to the trash can and slipped the flyer card in my purse.

Chapter 13

Evan

My mama's words about starting a family and living right echoed in my head even louder once I got released. I knew I could do it. The weed thing was just a stupid choice I made. I was never in trouble before, and I didn't plan to ever be in it again.

The past two weeks with Rocky had been fire, but I wished I was able to see her more. I knew she was all about getting her business off the ground, though, so I didn't stress her. She and her girl Layla was opening a freak school, and they were mad busy trying to get the place they leased ready for the grand opening party. Instead, I figured out that time was wasting and I needed to get everything rolling.

I was nervous about asking Rocky the big question, but I knew it was do or die. I almost punked out and decided to wait until after their business was up and running, but, damn, I felt some kind of fire inside my heart for the girl, and that shit was burning like a mug.

The ring I bought her wasn't fancy or anything, but I knew she'd understand that I was trying to pull myself outta the hole I'd been in. I brought a bottle of Patrón Silver (her favorite) to her crib that night and we ate some bomb-ass quesadillas she'd cooked up.

We were getting ready to make another batch of the margaritas, and I thought it would be the perfect time to ask the question that had been burning a hole in my brain the whole night.

"Rocky, we been knowing each other for a long time, but I feel like every day I see you is the first time. You make me feel fresh and new every day. So, baby, I want to know." I got down on one knee and pulled out the ring box. "Will you marry me?"

She looked like she'd seen a ghost. She was quiet for a few seconds, and then she said, "Evan, I appreciate this. I really do. But I can't get married right now."

I felt like someone had just taken a fuckin' knife and stabbed me in the heart.

"It's not you, sweetie. It's just that I have so much going on; so much on my plate right now I can't even think about getting married."

I took a long-ass breath and got up off the floor. I tried to understand where she was coming from, but it was hard as hell. All I knew was that I had just been shut the fuck down. I sat back in the chair and chewed on one of the ice cubes from my empty glass.

Then, she made it up to me.

She kneeled down between my legs, reached up for my glass and put one of the ice cubes in her mouth. Then she unzipped my pants and went to work on my dick. There were a whole bunch of sensations going through my body. Her wet mouth, the coldness of the ice, the warmth of her hands was all driving me crazy.

Then she did some shit I ain't never thought I would let anybody do. She pulled my pants down and told me to scoot to the edge of the chair. Then she started touching my ass. I have to admit, that shit felt kinda good. Even when I was locked up, I never let none of those muthafuckas get to me, so it was kirkin' me the hell out that I was letting her do what she did next. She took her pointing finger and stuck it in her mouth to get it all wet and warm. Then she put that shit up my asshole! No pun intended, but I was like 'what the fuck?'

She went back to work with her tongue, swirling around the head and then taking the whole thing in her mouth. Then something happened that I can't explain. It musta been the head. Yeah, it had to be the head. I swear I busted the hardest nut I ever busted. By that time, I'd forgot all about the ring and her saying no.

After a few minutes of getting myself together, I laid her on the table and licked her clit until she was breathing real heavy. That shit had me so fuckin' hard. When I put it in, she sucked in some breath and then opened her eyes to look at me. When I started pounding her, she closed her eyes again and started moaning. I was tickling her spot with my finger while I was pumping, and I could tell it was driving her bananas.

"Oh yeah, baby. Give me that big dick. Mmmm, Lucas."

The world stopped, her eyes flew open and I yelled, "What the fuck you just say?"

She smiled, all nervous and shit and said, "I said give me that big dick."

I pulled out of her. "No, you just said some other dude's

name. What the fuck is this, Rocky? You fucking around on me?"

She sat up. "No, no, of course not. I'm sorry, baby. Purple Lucas is my, ummm, vibrator's name. It's been just me and him for a while and I—"

"I don't believe this shit." I pulled up my pants and put my jacket on. "Where the fuck are my keys?"

"Come on, baby. Don't go. I swear to God, I'm telling the truth." She tried to stand in my way from getting into the living room.

"Bitch, get the fuck out my way," I said, pulling my keys out of my inside jacket pocket.

"Bitch? Who the fuck you calling a bitch? Get the fuck out you trifling-ass mother—"

"Whatever, I'm gone. Dirty ass ho."

I pulled out of my parking spot and drove about ninety on East West Highway until I saw flashing red and blue lights behind me.

Chapter 14

Layla

Raquelle and I were working on the final touches on the Freak In the Sheets Pleasure Institute, and I couldn't hide the smile that crept across my face when I thought about the phone conversation I had with Jabar the night before.

He and I had been having some great conversation for the last few nights. It was like there was some kind of instant connection there, but it included none of the superficial, cat-and-mouse type of stuff. We talked late into the night about the silliest things like movies, music, television (which I found out that I was way out of touch on), and crazy celebrities. He made me laugh so hard, I had tears running down my cheeks. Hunter definitely never did that, unless you count his golfing get-up.

We also talked about our families, and I came out and told him I was, in fact, the Lane he thought I was. It turned out he was from Atlanta originally, but moved to the DC area a few years ago to get his master's in Political Science. He figured it was the best place in the world to study politics. I had my doubts about that one.

"What are you grinning about?" Raquelle asked, snapping me out of my reverie.

The frown she had been wearing since we got there softened a little. She was sitting at the receptionist's desk working on her laptop, and I was hanging some sensual fabrics from the ceiling for an exotic effect. We had worked our magic on the building and it was fly enough to give Oprah's boy Nate a run for his money.

"Oh, nothing." I went back to my fabric stapling, but then couldn't take it anymore. "OK, I can't stand it. I met someone."

"Hmph. Someone? Like a guy?"

"Yeah, like a guy."

"And how long has this been going on?"

"Oh, not long. I met him the day I quit my job, but we just started talking."

She looked up from her laptop and put her funky pink glasses on top her head. "Go on, you little hoochie."

"Hoochie? Damn, Raq. We haven't even gone out. Not everyone moves as fast as your behind."

She waved her hand at me. "You know I'm messing with you. So, are you two going to go out or is this some sort of new telephone dating I'm not up on? You know I gots to stay on top of these things."

"Shut up. We're meeting for dinner tonight."

"OK, that's better." She sighed and looked at the laptop screen again.

"You going to tell me what's going on with you? You've had that funky look on your face since we got here."

She shrugged. "Not much to tell. Oh, except Evan proposed to me last night. I turned him down, gave him some crazy head, and then called out your brother's name."

The power stapler dropped out of my hand, missing my toe by mere inches. "You did what?"

She covered her face with her hands. "Yeah, you heard me right." She sighed and picked up her cell phone. "He's been trying to call me since late last night, but I haven't picked up. Part of me thinks I did it on purpose. Maybe I was trying to make him leave. He said some foul shit to me, though."

"Why? I thought things were going well?" I turned off the air compressor that turned staples into missiles and stood in front of the desk.

"It was. I mean, I guess it was. I'm just not sure I still love him. I think it's like a pity party."

"Pity party?"

"Yeah, I guess I feel bad for what happened to his mother and the fact that I left him hanging in prison. Oh, but the sex is still good except for that little mishap last night."

"Well then. So what now?"

"I don't have the energy to think about it right now. I want to put all my focus into this place." She placed the cell phone back on the desk. "I don't need any distractions right now."

"I hear you."

Since I knew Jabar, but didn't really *know him* know him, I told him to meet me at Il Mulino, which he chose, I might add. He asked me my top three cuisines and came up with the new Italian place on Vermont Avenue. I had eaten at the New York location, so I was ready to get down with some of their caramel cheesecake.

I dressed simply, but, at Raquelle's suggestion, I kicked it up a notch and showed a little cleavage. She was always telling me to use what I got. Meaning, my impressive C cups. I wore a navy blue wrap dress, some simple silver hoops with sapphires around them, a small silver snake chain, my hair off my neck, and my new navy Taryn Rose heels. I thought I looked pretty hot, but not slutty. The shoes added a little sexy innocence.

I walked into the dimly lit restaurant and about ten seconds later Jabar walked in behind me.

"I thought that was you." He smiled and kissed me on the cheek. "You look beautiful."

"Thanks. You look pretty good yourself."

He was dressed nice, but casual in some black slacks and a black and green striped shirt. I could smell his cologne, and it kind of made me want to bite into his neck like a vampire.

I didn't know where those feelings were coming from, but I kind of liked it. He smiled and walked me over to the hostess, who sat us at a quaint table against the back wall of the restaurant. The candlelight was reflecting in his eyes, and it took him glancing down at my menu and back at me to tell me that I was staring.

We selected a wine from the list and placed our orders. While we waited, the silence was easy and a little comforting. We made light conversation as we ate, and we decided to share the notorious cheesecake. It was a sensual act, our forks kind of meeting in this forbidden place. OK, so maybe I just wanted him.

He walked me out to my car and frowned. "You need to wash this thing." He took his finger and touched my dusty Acura.

I laughed. "Look at you. Telling me what to do already." I winked. "I've just been busy with the business."

He nodded.

I felt a little chilly, so I asked him to join me in the car. He agreed and we got in and I turned on the motor to start the heater. My Willie Max CD started playing, and by chance, "Can't Get Enough" happened to be on. The last thing I needed was encouragement for the sexual energy I was already feeling. I reached to change the CD.

"Hey, I like that song. I never heard anything else out of them, but that was a tight song. Raphael Saadiq did his thing on that one."

I was surprised he'd ever heard of them. I was a one-hit wonder junkie, and it always excited me when someone actually recognized one of those groups or singers that disappeared off the face of the earth. Lucas teased me about it all the time, saying I was probably the only one who bought most of the CDs I owned.

I leaned my head back on the headrest and tried to let the music relax me. The tension was building, and if I didn't get Jabar out of my car soon, I was going to do something I would regret.

"What are you thinking about?" he asked.

I raised my head and turned to look at him. I wanted to say, "You and me in a hot shower," but instead I played it safe. "Oh, I was just thinking that it's getting late and I have to be up early tomorrow to prepare for the grand opening."

That was when he leaned in and kissed me like I haven't been kissed since high school. In fact, I was feeling a lot like a horny teenager. When his moist lips touched mine, I felt a tingle between my legs.

He cupped the side of my face with his slightly rough, manly hand and it was a little too much for me. I was getting those butterfly feelings, and I had promised myself this wouldn't be a rebound relationship. We were just having fun, right? Like Raquelle had said, we didn't need any major distractions.

I pulled away. "Jabar, I can't—"

He looked into my eyes. He looked down for a moment and then said, "I want to see you again."

"OK," I said, although I knew I shouldn't have. I was already feeling too much too soon, and I didn't really even know this man.

"Great," he said.

He raised my hand to his lips and said, "Good night," before exiting the car.

I didn't answer until after he had closed the door. "Yes, it was."

Chapter 15

Lucas

I felt like a weight had been lifted off my shoulders after I broke it off with Catalina. Part of it was the fact that I didn't have to worry about a wedding, a commitment, and somewhat of a trophy wife. The other part of it was that I was finally free to tell Raquelle how I really felt about her. I'd heard from my sister that she and the thug guy had broken up, and I finally felt like it was time to make my move.

But first, I had to figure out what was going on with Jay-Ron. He still hadn't shown up for school or lessons, and it was going on a month. I was apprehensive about visiting his stomping grounds once again, but this time I felt like I was a little more prepared. I had switched cars with Raleigh. I figured his '02 Envoy was a lot less inconspicuous than my Jag. I also lost the khakis and polo and opted for some casual jeans and a Sean Jean jacket.

I headed back to Green Bay and was surprised to see Jay-Ron standing outside with a few scraggly looking people around.

I parked Raleigh's car and was about to get out when Jay-Ron met me at the driver's side door.

"Mr. Lane, what you doing here?"

"Do you really need to ask me that question?"

He dropped his head back and then sighed. "Man, come on."

We went up the too-familiar pissy elevator to his apartment. Once again, the place was spotless.

"You here all by yourself again?"

"Yeah, Nikki's out somewhere with Ace."

"Who is this Ace guy anyway?"

Jay-Ron looked like he was debating with himself over whether to fill me in. After I took a seat on the worn out flowered sofa, he realized I wasn't going anywhere until I got some answers. He pulled one of the chairs from the kitchen table and sat down.

"I lied to you about something," he said.

"What?"

"My mother didn't die of breast cancer."

"She didn't?"

"Nope. And she didn't die last year, either."

I didn't know where this was going. "No?"

"She died like four years ago. And I don't know how she died. I found her one morning in her bed. I called 911, but it was too late. They said she died of natural causes, but I don't believe that."

"Why?"

"I can't really explain it. I just know."

"OK."

"Nikki told me Mama had life insurance, and that's why we was living pretty good for a while. She starting bringing Ace around. But then the money pretty much ran out, and we was scraping by. She told me he was gonna take care of us, but she basically just moved out and left me here. I been here for like two years by myself. She shows up every once in a while, but it just me mostly." He looked around the apartment, his thin shoulders shrugging. "So, I have to do what I have to do to survive. I figured out I couldn't depend on her for anything."

"I'm sorry you had to go through all that."

"Ay, it ain't no thing. There's people out there that got it a lot worse than me."

I was feeling spoiled and a little guilty. "What can I do?"

"Ain't nothing for you to do. You done enough already." He got up and got a photo album off the shelf. He opened it up to the first page. "This was my ma when she was young. She won the citywide science fair." He pointed to a black and white newspaper clipping with a teenaged girl. He read the caption. "Yasmeen Young of Branch Avenue, SE wins Citywide Science Fair."

Something struck me about that name, but I couldn't put my finger on it. Just when it seemed like it was coming to me, there was a loud knock on the door.

"Jay-Ron. Open up, young'en."

Jay-Ron looked a little panicked as he quickly replaced the album on the shelf and went to the door.

"What's good, Ace?"

So that was the infamous Ace. He really didn't look too scary. He wasn't much bigger than I was, but he had a weird fire in his eyes.

"Who dis?" He eyeballed me and furrowed his brow.

Jay-Ron shifted his cap on his head. "That's my teacher. He's cool."

Ace didn't say anything. He just nodded once, and he and

Jay-Ron disappeared into what I assumed was the bedroom. After a few minutes ago, I heard their voices raise a little. I stood, a little alarmed that Jay-Ron might need my help.

"Everything okay in there?" I asked.

The door flew open and Ace came out. "Man, stay the fuck out my bidness fo' I have to get in yours." He looked back into the bedroom. "Don't fuck wit' me, young."

He exited the apartment and Jay-Ron still didn't come out. I walked back to his bedroom doorway and saw him sitting on the bed analyzing something in Ziploc baggies. When he saw me, he quickly hid them behind his back.

"You want to talk about it?"

"Nah, man. Just get out of here before you get me killed or get your shoes dirty." He got up and closed the bedroom door in my face.

Chapter 16

Raquelle

The grand opening was a big affair, and we had close to a hundred and fifty people in the lobby, taking tours of our facilities. I had arranged for the caterer to bring an impressive spread of erotic foods. She had done it up with chocolate covered strawberries, an array of fruits, a pomegranate punch, and an avocado dip with thin slices of French bread.

I also had an open bar set up serving two brand new cocktails I had concocted: the Freak in the Sheets Martini and the Lady in the Streets Margarita. They seemed to be going over pretty well, because everyone was laughing and interacting, and the line at the bar was pretty long.

I went over to the bartender I had hired to check on her. She had her long black hair up in a high ponytail and was wearing the company colors: blue and black.

"You doing OK over here, Octavia?"

She blew some air out of her mouth. "Yeah, but, girl, these

drinks must be pretty good because the same people keep lining up."

I laughed. "Well, good. I'm going to send one of the servers over here to give you a hand."

She gave me an appreciative smile. "Thanks, Miss Scott."

Layla had brought her new friend Jabar and Lucas was there with his drummer. Every time I looked at Lucas he was looking at me. He'd act like he was caught and then just smile.

I announced that registration was officially open and within moments, all seven of the laptops we had set up for online registration were in use. I was also taking down some registrations by hand, but it got to be too much so I called Layla over to give me a hand.

After another twenty minutes, I saw one of the last people on earth I wanted to see.

"Sierra. How are you?" Layla asked.

Sierra looked at her and gave her what I would almost swear was a seductive smile. "Layla. Nice place. Can I sign up for some courses?"

Layla looked at me and I shrugged.

"Sure," she said. "Which ones were you interested in registering for?"

Sierra emptied the rest of her cocktail. "I'd like to sign up for the How To Please a Woman class."

Layla's eyes got wide, and I couldn't help but smile. I wasn't going to judge the girl, though. Sexual liberation is good in most forms.

Layla furiously flipped through the list of courses. "We have a class this coming Monday."

Sierra licked her lips. "Perfect. Sign me up, beautiful."

I must have missed something in the four minutes it took me to sign up the next guy in line for the Multiple Male Orgasms class, because when I looked up, Sierra had Layla in a lip lock.

A split second later, Layla pulled back and took off out of the lobby.

"Here's my registration fee." Sierra handed me $100 and then winked.

I scanned the room to see if Jabar or Lucas had seen what just went down. I saw Lucas making his way through the crowd.

"What was that all about?" he asked after he had finally made his way to me.

"Search me. Hey, since you're up here, you think you could help me get these folks registered so I can get them cleared out and see where Layla ran off to?"

"Anything for you," he said, giving me a wink.

"Wow, two winks in less than two minutes."

He and I worked for the next 40 minutes and shortly thereafter, the crowd had considerably thinned. I informed the remaining guests to help themselves to the food and drink before I took off to see about my girl.

I finally found her in the private admin office near the back of the building. When I spotted her, she was leaning forward with her elbows on the desk and her head in her hands.

"What just happened out there?"

She looked up at me with a worried look plastered on her face. "I have no idea. Did Jabar see that? Oh, God. What about Lucas?"

"I don't know where Jabar went, but Lucas saw it. He's

worried about you. What the hell is up with Sierra? Has she lost her damn mind?"

"Oh, God. This is too much." She lowered her head back into her hands.

"Why would she even come here?

"She said she's not friends with Catalina anymore. She said Catalina has gone off the deep end and basically disappeared." Her face turned from worry to reflection before she said, "And then she kissed me."

I exhaled a long breath and pondered it all for a minute. "I just can't figure out why she would do that. What the hell did you two say to each other while I was registering my guy?"

"She just said she has always found me attractive and then moved in for the lip derby."

Layla looked like she was going to cry, but instead she started laughing uncontrollably. I couldn't help but contribute a chuckle or two.

"Remind me to put a three drink limit on folks next time. Fucking lushes."

The laughter started again.

"Wanna hear something ever crazier?"

I didn't know if I could handle much more. "Uh, sure."

"I actually kinda liked it." She sighed and returned her head to her hands.

Chapter 17

Evan

It'd been a week since Rocky and I had that fight. It turned out the cops weren't after me. I slowed down and they flew past me. I got tired of hearing the same voicemail message on Rocky's phone for a week straight, and I kept thinking about that crazy shit that happened. I kept calling her because I kinda felt bad about saying those things to her, plus I loved her and I was willing to trust and forgive if she would just hear me out. Anyway, she never picked up or returned my calls, so I got a little siced and decided to go to the strip club to release some of the stress, even though I avoided those places most of the time. It seems like trouble follows strip clubs, and trouble was the last thing I needed. I ain't really want to run into anyone I knew from around the way. I'd been laying mad low trying to get myself on track.

Chica's wasn't an upscale club, but it wasn't a dirty hood club either. The girls were freaky, but they weren't busted like the place in Northeast where the chicks were all scarred up and shit.

I was sitting at one of the tables in the front of the club so I could get the best view. I had a stack of cash and two Courvoisiers sitting on my table, and I was ready to see some titties and ass.

The DJ took it back and put on the New Jack joint, "Booty Call," and these two girls came out wearing some black leather bikinis. They were doing their thing, but I was more interested in the honey that was giving this white dude a lap dance. She didn't really look like she belonged in a strip club. Her face was twisted up a little, and it looked like she didn't want to be doing what she was doing. That shit made me look at strippers different. I would put money down that most of 'em didn't want to do what they was doing.

I motioned for the waitress to come over. She was a cute Hispanic girl with big titties and some thick-ass legs.

"How can I help you?" She was trying to sound all sexy, but it came off kinda fake.

I nodded to the out of place-looking lap dancer. "Tell her I'm next."

"You mean Kitty?" She nodded and went over to the chick and whispered something in her ear. Then she went to take care of her next customer.

I was eyeballing Kitty, and she caught me staring. She changed her expression from looking fed up to acting like she was all into grinding on that dirty dude. I turned back to the stage, where the girls were now feeling on each other and untying each other's tops. I was close enough that I could smell the leather.

"You called?"

I looked to my left and saw the Kitty standing there. She placed her hand on my shoulder.

"Yeah, ma. I wanted my turn." I looked her up from her red high heels to her short red skirt and then I stopped, wondering what her pussy looked like. I wondered if she had the kitty cat porn pussy, the bald, barely-legal pussy, the butterfly pussy, the African bush pussy, or the fat clit, juicy lips, little hole pussy like Rocky.

I bought her a drink and handed her the fee for the lap dance and she went to work. She kind of smelled like what you smell when you walk by the counter at Nordstrom. She bent forward and I could see that she was a butterfly. Her lips were sticking out of her red thong.

It was fucked up, but I wasn't even getting hard.

"Ay, baby. Sit down and have your drink with me."

She straightened up looked kinda confused but relieved at the same time.

"My name's Evan, what's yours?"

"Kitty."

We started talking about whatever I wanted to talk about, and before I knew it, I was out of cash and the club was calling for last call.

"What you doing after this?"

She looked like she didn't know how to answer that. "Going home, I guess."

"Where your man at?"

Her face told me that I had hit a nerve. At first she looked kinda hurt, but then her grill went ice.

"I don't have one."

"Aight then, that makes two of us."

"Wait outside. I'm going to go back and change and then I'll be out."

I was blown by how easy that shit was. I didn't really want

to fuck her, but if it came to that, I wasn't going to turn her ass down. I thought about Rocky for a minute, but then I pushed it out of my mind. She showed me what she really thought about me after she didn't even return my calls. Shit, she should have been the one begging me. Not the other way around.

I was only waiting a few minutes before she came out the front door. She looked even more out of place once she had changed. She was now wearing a short, frilly, peach, Paris Hilton looking dress and carrying one of those crazy looking pocketbooks with the fur and leather and shit on it.

I rolled down my window and waved to her. She got in the car and I asked her where she wanted to go.

"Let's go to the Ritz."

"Damn, girl. You got Ritz money?"

She looked deep in thought for a few seconds and then changed her mind. "OK. The Doubletree."

I checked in at the front desk while she went to the gift shop, and we went up the elevator to the sixth floor in silence. She wouldn't even make eye contact with me.

We got to the room and she went straight to the bathroom. I kicked off my shoes and sat down on the bed and clicked on the TV.

She came out a few minutes later and said, "So how do you want to do this? Do you want to be on top?"

I just shook my head and laughed. "Nah, just lay back for a while." She shrugged and sat on the other edge of the bed.

"You're new at this, ain't you?"

"New at what?" She was trying to sound like I had offended her, but I knew I hit the nail on the head.

"The dancing, leaving with strange men thing. You know."

"You aren't that strange. We talked for a long time, and I would know if you were a nut."

I laughed. "Not really."

She shrugged and looked around the room.

"What's your story? Why you working at Chica's?"

"Why does anybody work there? Because they like it? Because they think it's exciting to grind on perverts? No. Just like everyone else, I work there because I need the money."

"Aight, shorty. Don't flip on me."

She rolled her eyes. "So what's your story? Why are you paying for sex?"

"Whoa, who said anything about paying for sex?"

"Well, that is why we're here isn't it?"

"I don't know about you, but I thought we was just relaxing and getting to know each other."

"Oh, God." She smacked herself in the forehead.

"And if you wanna know my story, I just got out of prison a few weeks ago, the woman I love just turned my proposal down, and she called out another dude's name while we was fuckin'."

"Damn. I thought my life was messed up." She got a strange look on her face. "Wait, did you just say you were in prison?"

I got up and went over to the mini-bar to see what kind of poison was in there. I knew this was about to get deep.

"Yeah, that's what I said."

"Oh, God. I'm in a hotel room with an ex-con I don't even know. Oh, God. Oh God."

"Calm down, shorty. I ain't no murderer or rapist or nothing like that. I was locked up for weed."

She seemed to relax a little. Then her eyes got wide. "That's it. You can help me. Oh, yes!"

I raised an eyebrow. "Help you with what?"

"You and your convict friends can kill him."

"Whoa. What the fuck you talking about?"

She stood up and gathered her jacket and weird-ass pocketbook. "I would like to hire you to kill my father."

I knew the bitch was crazy then. "Hell nah. I ain't killing nobody."

"Well, it doesn't have to be you. I just want you to broker the deal. There's a million dollars in it for you and your professional if you can get the job done."

Damn, a million dollars was enough to start completely new in a different city without having to worry about shit.

"I don't know." I started to rack my brain for people I knew who would be down. I wasn't sure I'd be able to find anyone to do the deed, and I sure as hell didn't want to be the one to have to do it.

"Give me your number. I will be in touch about this." She picked up the phone on the desk, punched the front desk button, and said, "Yes, can you please call me a cab?" She hung up and fixed herself to leave.

I wrote my number on a piece of the hotel notepaper and handed it to her.

"Got it. I'll be in touch about that thing we talked about." She opened the door.

This shit had taken a weird turn, but I couldn't do nothing but go with the flow at that point.

"Before you go, there's something I forgot to ask you."

She turned around. "What?"

"Don't get all excited. I just want to know your name."

She looked a little scared. "Well, they call me Kitty at Chica's."

"Nah, I know that. I want to know your real name. If you know my name and we been talking 'bout what we been talking about, I want your real name."

She sighed and rolled her eyes. Before the door closed, I heard her say, "Catalina. That's all you need to know."

Chapter 18

Raquelle

When it was all said and done, our courses were booked up for the next month, and I was excited to get it all started. We had even snagged a private erotic dance course for Chica's Gentleman's Club. All their dancers were going to be learning some of the latest techniques from our dance instructor, Jalina.

Jalina was a Brazilian gem we found through craigslist. We placed an ad and she was the first to respond. When she came in for her audition and a quickie lesson for me and Layla, we really didn't need to see anyone else. She worked it out with moves neither of us had ever seen and her exotic features and curves were appealing for anyone to watch. I had a feeling the dancers at Chica's would be paying close attention to her lessons.

I had scheduled the Sex Toy Basics course in the Velvet Lounge room. There were four overstuffed purple velvet sofas and three red velvet chaise lounges that formed a semi-circle. I had a low demonstration table set up with various toys from Infatuation, a sex toy company we had partnered with. I had the items arranged in the order I was going to speak about them.

I also had our anatomically correct love mannequins, Denise and Lenny, positioned on a chaise next to the table. They both looked like they were ready to get it on.

I looked around the room to determine what kind of audience I would be speaking to, but I had learned a long time ago that looks could be deceiving. There was a good mix of people in attendance. There were three blonde soccer moms who sat together sipping the plum wine that came complimentary with registration on one sofa. Next to them was a Bootsy Collins look-alike (if Bootsy had ever worn velour sweat suits) who was sipping his wine out of an encrusted goblet that looked like he stole it from Li'l Jon.

I started out by introducing myself and giving them a little overview of what we'd be discussing. I had been taught in school to keep things fairly clinical in the educational setting, so I opted to use the anatomical names for the male and female body parts rather than the slang terms.

"I hope you are all comfortable and ready to learn." I saw some smiles pop up around the room, but they were outnumbered by looks of sheer terror.

"Firstly, I wanted to lead you in a relaxation exercise.

I held up a vibrating cock ring.

"Who knows what this is?"

Bootsy smiled so big, his gold tooth caught the light and nearly blinded me. No one said anything.

"OK. This is a vibrating cock ring. It has two uses. It's very flexible and soft." I demonstrated by placing the cock ring on Lenny's penis. "The vibration side can be placed on top or on bottom, for either clitoral or anal and testicular stimulation." I moved the ring from the top to the bottom. I heard a few "Oh's."

"Also, some people say it helps the male hold his erection for a longer period of time."

I put the cock ring back on the table and moved on down the line.

"These are anal beads. I'll give you one guess where these are supposed to go."

Light chuckles echoed throughout the audience. I used Denise for this demo.

"Would anyone like to try these?"

No one said a word, but I noticed one of the soccer moms had a slight smile creeping into the corners of her mouth.

I looked at her and said, "Anyone?"

She raised her hand bashfully.

"Great. Come on up. First I will demonstrate a few techniques and then you can try." I flashed her a smile.

I knelt in front of Denise and positioned her legs in a way that would give me easier access to her anus.

"First of all, make sure your partner is primed and lubed. Primed can mean just foreplay with gentle teasing in the anal area. Before you go too deep, however, make sure to apply some silicone lube to the area."

I got the small black bottle of Moist from the table and held it up for the class to see.

"Silicone lubes are great because they don't lose their slickness. Oh, and they don't cause problems with the pH of the vagina like some of the flavored lubes. They're safe for use with condoms as well. You should always use a lube for anal play."

I dripped a couple of drops of the lube onto my fingers and applied it to the anal beads.

"Now, this large ring at the end of the beads is basically to keep them from getting lost. Since the purpose of anal beads is to stimulate the sphincter, they should be inserted slowly."

I began by slowly inserting the first bead, and then the second, and so on until they were completely submerged.

"You don't have to go all the way in. The key is to try it out and see what you like."

I turned to the soccer mom. "Would you like to try now?"

She nodded and then I guided her to try out the beads on Lenny.

"Now a lot of people want to know when the best time to take out the beads is. I say, whenever you want. You can slowly pull them out right after insertion and then repeat the process, or you or your partner can pull them out right before climax. It's a personal preference, as are most things related to sex."

I went on to some more toys, including a double-ended dong, butterfly clit stimulator, male masturbators, and the butt plug. Then I brought out the big guns.

I had a Monkey Rocker and a Je Joue that I knew was going to blow their minds. I walked over to the Monkey Rocker, which I had covered with a pink satin sheet. I paused for effect and then revealed the contraption.

"Now how many of you know what this is?"

There was dead silence in the room and their eyes all looked like deer in headlights.

"This, my friends, is a monkey rocker. It's the safest sex partner you'll ever find. Unless, of course, you bounce too hard on it and break it." I winked.

The Monkey Rocker was a bench-like piece of furntiture

that stood about three feet high. It had a place to attach dongs, and there were several positions you could use to get the boat rocking nicely. I demonstrated first using Denise, showing the students the woman-on-top position. I then demonstrated how different positions could be achieved.

I also introduced the Je Joue to them. It was a vibrator that could be connected to a computer and different groove patterns could be downloaded to it. I could tell by the dumbfounded looks on their faces that that toy was better suited for the intermediate class, so I wrapped things up and asked them if there were any questions. No one answered. They seemed a little scared.

"Yeah, baby, I gots me a queshon 'bout dem anus beads." Bootsy stood up and pointed to the anal beads. "Do ya hafta buy dem kind of beads, or can we just use some of the big fat necklaces my mama left me in her will?"

I heard a few snickers in the room, and it took everything I had to control my own urge to laugh.

"Umm, it's really better to get the beads that were specifically made for that purpose." I paused. "For ummm, sanitary reasons."

"I gotcha, baby."

"Any other questions?"

A petite young black woman in the back raised her hand and I nodded for her to speak.

"What if you're too short to reach the floor on that Monkey Rocker?"

I smiled. "Why not slip on a pair of stilettos and put even more fantasy into action? Or you can use some yoga blocks or books."

"Thanks."

"Anyone else?" I scanned the room, but there was no answer. "OK, well, please check your emails for a class evaluation. We're anxious to hear your feedback."

The students filed out of the room, and I had officially completed the first class at Freak in the Sheets Pleasure Institute. I went out front where Layla was sitting at the reception desk.

"How'd it go?"

"Interesting, very interesting. I think I'm going to like this."

She smiled and grabbed her purse and we hurried out to grab some lunch at the Chinese place down the block since I only had an hour before my 2:00 P.M. Blow Job Basics class, and I had some things I wanted to go over with Marguerite, the other instructor I had hired. We went to school together, and she had the same degree as I did. She, however, had experience in an area I didn't. She was a transsexual.

Chapter 19

Layla

A-Train, hadn't been invited back to Takoma Station, but Lucas was able to secure some new gigs around the area in the meantime. After the last class let out, Raquelle, Jabar, and I went to grab some dinner and then were on our way to Jimmy's Spot in Temple Hills, Maryland on a Saturday night to hear them. Raquelle was in the back seat of my Acura singing along with 702, and Jabar just had this sexy smile plastered on his face. I hadn't seen him since the night of the crazy grand opening a week earlier, and I think he was just happy to be around me. The feeling was mutual.

Jabar thought Freak in the Sheets was a really cool idea. He loved that we were helping people to free themselves. I hesitated telling him the nature of the business for a while, because I didn't want him to think I was a freak and he was going to get in the panties right away. When I told Lucas about the place and what it was about, his eyes nearly jumped out of their sockets. But that could have been more of a fantasy about Raquelle. I knew they had it bad for each other, and I was going to see to it that they got together one way or another. But anyway, it was cool that they both showed up at the grand opening to show their support.

Some people might think that I was basically financing someone else's dream, but it wasn't like that. I was actually really passionate about the business. I was learning a lot from just being there, and one thing I learned was that I was a little more sexually curious than I had originally thought. Most of my sexual experience consisted of me and a guy rolling around for a few minutes until he got his rocks off. Raquelle always told me sex was a fun and liberating experience, but I just didn't see it. However, when Freak in the Sheets opened, it was like my mind opened along with it and I wasn't as much of a sexual prude.

We went into the club, and A-Train was already in full swing with one of their original songs. The crowd was older and pretty laid back. The place was a hole in the wall, but they were known for their live music.

"I think he reserved us a table," I said to Raquelle and Jabar. They nodded and followed me to the second row of tables where the reserved sign sat on the table in the center. I was cool with it, because that meant Raquelle and Lucas could make lovey eyes at each other while Jabar and I chilled.

We sat down and ordered our drinks, and the waitress was back in what seemed like seconds. I took a sip of my caramel apple martini. I had decided I was going to drink chick drinks that night.

I looked toward the dance floor, and I couldn't believe my eyes. Temple Hills and Jimmy's Spot was the last place I expected to see Hunter Baldwin. I saw him coming my way and jumped up from the table before he could come over and make a scene in front of Jabar.

"Layla." He sighed.

I looked around nervously. "Hunter, this isn't the place."

"I don't want any trouble. I just want to talk to you. I've missed you."

"I'm with someone." I looked back at the table where Raquelle and Jabar were sitting.

"Oh. I saw Raquelle and assumed . . ."

"No, he's with me. Look, I know it's hard to understand, but it's really and truly over between us. I wish you could see that."

He looked like he was going to cry, but then he straightened his shoulders and glanced back over at Jabar. "I think I see it pretty clearly now."

"Good. I wish you the best."

"Yeah." He turned and went toward the bar instead of toward the exit.

"Great." I went back to the table to join Jabar and Raquelle. She shot me a look and I nodded. She was asking me if everything was cool, and I let her know it was. Jabar said nothing; he just scooted my chair closer to his. I found it to be sort of cute. Hunter was sitting at the bar, trying not to be obvious, but he was still staring. It was making me kind of nervous.

"Want to dance?" I asked Jabar.

He smiled. "Sure."

We went up to the crowded dance floor and found a nice spot in the corner. A-Train was working it out with their own spin on "Cococure" by Maxwell.

Jabar had his right arm securely wrapped around my waist, and I just let myself go with his flow. He had pretty good rhythm, and I wondered what else he would be good at. It was hot up there on the dance floor; I felt a bead of sweat run down my forehead as the beat continued to pulse. My green and brown baby doll top was starting to stick to my skin. He pulled me in so his lips were close to my ear. I didn't know if my breathing was so heavy because of the dancing or because I wanted to kiss him so bad. But I didn't think I could do that; not with all those people around.

But I surprised myself. I looked over and an attractive couple were already going at it. The sight of them turned me on even more, and when I felt Jabar's hand slide down to my hips, I pulled back so we were face to face with our noses touching. I could feel his sweet breath against my lips, and I couldn't take it any longer.

I let my lips softly graze across his, but then it was like something else took over, and we were in a full out lip lock. I heard a low moan hum through his lips, and at that moment, I knew there was more than sweat between my legs making me wet. We were caught in a reverie of pure desire, and then, the music suddenly stopped and I heard my brother announce a set break. We stood there for a moment, seemingly trying to determine what had just happened.

"That was nice," I said.

He smiled. "Mmm. Nice wasn't the word I was going to pick, but I'll take it."

We went back to the table, where Lucas and Raquelle were sitting. Raquelle mouthed the word "hoochie," and I couldn't help but laugh.

"Jabar, this is my brother and the band leader of A-Train, Lucas Lane. Lucas, this is Jabar Cardell."

"Nice to meet you, man. Y'all were killing it up there." They pounded fists.

"Thanks, man. You two seemed to be enjoying the Maxwell selection."

I kicked him.

"Whew, I need some water. Can I interest anyone in anything from the bar?" Jabar asked.

"Water would be great," I said.

"I'm good, man." Lucas said.

"No thanks," Raquelle answered.

I admired that rear view I loved so much as he made his way over to the bar. I looked around for Hunter, but figured he had left after seeing our display on the dance floor.

Raquelle and Lucas were jabbering about something, but I was too focused on Jabar. I saw him coming back our way with two bottles of water in his hands when Hunter stepped up behind him and tapped him on the shoulder.

Before I could move, Hunter had cold-cocked Jabar in the jaw. I had no idea he could throw a punch like that.

Jabar threw a right, smashing Hunter in the nose.

"Lucas," I screamed, pointing to the two men. "Do something."

"Aww, damn. Why is it every time you come to a show . . ." He took off and arrived at the tussle about the same time the security guy did. I went over to the crowd of people standing around them.

"Move back. Everybody move back," the bouncer said.

He grabbed Hunter by his shirt, which was now bloody from the gushing from his nose, and said, "I'm going to have to ask you to leave, sir."

"Yeah, yeah." Hunter straightened his clothes and left after shooting me a look of death.

I went over to Jabar and lightly touched his face. "I'm so sorry."

He shook his head. "It's not your fault. I take it that was your ex-fiancé?"

"Yeah. I swear I had no idea he would be here."

He sniffed and put his arm around my shoulder. "Don't worry about it. I'd probably go crazy if I had a woman like you and messed it up too."

Back at the table, Raquelle was sitting there like a little kid.

"I didn't want to get involved. I been thrown out of enough clubs in the past few months, and I'm supposed to be a lady in the streets."

"It's OK," Jabar said, taking a long drink of the water he had originally set out to get. He looked at me. "If you don't mind, I think I had better get going. If you want to stay, I can definitely call a cab."

I looked at Raquelle and seized the moment to get those two together. "Give me a second."

I went over to the stage, where Lucas was trying to calm down and prepare for the final set of the evening.

"Lucas."

"I tell you, all the hateration. What the hell was Hunter doing here?"

"I have no idea." I looked at the floor. "Hey, I want to leave and take Jabar home. Do you think you could give Raquelle a ride? I think she was wanting to stay for the last set."

His face lit up and then he cleared his throat. "Oh yeah. I mean, sure, Sis, I can take her home."

I shook my head, but inside I was cheering for one small victory. "Ok then, love you."

"Love you too."

Jabar and I left. Raquelle was fine with catching a ride home with Lucas. Mmmhmm. I bet she was.

Jabar asked me to come inside when we pulled up to his

place in Lanham. I thought back to the erotic dance we shared earlier and agreed.

His place wasn't too bad for a bachelor pad. He had a pretty nice setup with hardwood floors, a brown leather sofa, and an entertainment center with enough electronic equipment to open up a Best Buy.

"Make yourself comfortable. I'm gonna go jump in the shower and get all this blood off me."

"OK, Superman." I winked. I browsed his CD collection, looking for any one-hit wonders I recognized. "Aww, damn. Vybe? I thought I was the only one who bought that CD." I laughed and continued browsing until I came across a CD that was lying face down on top of the rest of the jewel cases. I flipped it over and it turned out to be a DVD.

"Big Butt Slumber Party? Oh no he didn't."

"What didn't I do?" he came out smiling with no shirt and some drawstring pants.

I hid the DVD behind my back. "Oh, umm, I couldn't believe you had the Vybe CD."

He came over to where I was. "Oh yeah. They were pretty good. What ever happened to them?"

"No idea."

His eyes seemed to be scanning for something. "You didn't find a stray disc anywhere did you?"

"Stray disc? Umm, you mean *Big Butt Slumber Party?*" I whipped the DVD in front of his face and busted out laughing at the look of guilt, shame, and embarrassment on his face. The fact that I was laughing seemed to ease him a little.

"Layla, I'm sorry. I should've put that away or something."

I swatted him. The breeze it created sent the scent of his

body was my way. I was starting to have those vampire thoughts again.

"Don't be sorry. It's not that strange, you know."

"I know, it's just that I don't want you to get the wrong impression of me. I really like you and—"

"Can we watch it now?" I have no idea where that came from, but sweet little Layla felt like being naughty.

"Are you for real?"

"Yeah. For real."

He smiled. "You are something else, Layla Lane. One in a million."

I laughed. "No, I'm just tired of playing the innocent role all the time. Now this doesn't mean we're going to do anything."

"Of course not."

He dimmed the lights. "Do you want something to drink? Beer? Wine? Soda?"

"Soda's fine."

"OK, I'll be right back."

He returned with our drinks and popped the DVD in the player before turning on about a million different components. He fast-forwarded through all the phone sex commercials at the beginning and stopped on the menu.

"Select a scene or straight through?"

"Let's live a little and watch it straight through."

"As you wish."

I never knew that the porn experience could be enhanced so greatly. The surround sound, digital audio, and big screen made it seem like we were in the room watching those girls get it on with each other.

"Why do guys like to watch lesbians?"

He laughed. "I don't know. Maybe we're trying to get tips.

Or maybe it's just the fact that there's more than one naked girl at a time."

"Makes sense."

The sight of three voluptuous babes feeling, licking, kissing, poking, and spanking each other was turning me on more than I cared to admit. My thoughts went to Sierra and the kiss she gave me at the party. I wondered what it would be like to do some of the things I was watching with her.

Chapter 20

Catalina

I tried to come up with ways to ruin that black-hemian bitch Raquelle and get Lucas back, but I was on my own. Sierra wouldn't return my calls, and I really didn't have anyone else to help me design a plan. I fantasized about spiking the punch at her grand opening party with some kind of sedative or setting fire to the building and destroying the place. Reality waltzed back in, though, when my father called to find out how I planned to come up with the money. I decided one of the best places to find myself a sugar daddy would be at a gentlemen's club, so I looked into a few before determining that Chica's would be the most inconspicuous of the bunch. I was nervous about taking my clothes off in front of perfect strangers, but decided that I needed to use my perfect body to pay for itself.

I figured out that dancing stark naked wasn't the hardest part of working at Chica's. The trickiest part was keeping your identity a secret. I had been working there for a week or so before I met Evan, but in that week, I dodged a few old classmates and even the husbands of some of my mother's friends. Who knew Chica's was the go-to place?

It was around ten-thirty on a weeknight when my father came to the club. At first I didn't know for sure if it was him because he was turned to the side and it was pretty dark in there. But after he moved his head into the light, I was certain.

I nearly killed myself leaping over the empty table that stood between me and the door that led to the backstage area. I ran over and hid myself in the shadows of the door before peeking into the main club area to see just what he was up to.

It seemed like all the girls knew him; they were all flocking around him and he was eating up the attention. I had come to understand that men liked attention, whether it was from a stripper or their mother, but that wasn't what infuriated me about the situation. After a young dancer named Gigi was called to come out, my father took post near the stage, watching her every move as she swayed her hips to "Before I Let Go." Within a few moments, he pulled out a stack of cash and rained those bills on that dirty skank.

I wasn't angry for the reason you might think, however. I could care less about him being in a strip joint watching amateurs dance when he had a beautiful dancer at home. No, I was raging because he was giving so freely to a stripper and he was giving me ultimatums about money. Apparently, he didn't need it as badly as he relayed to me.

I got an idea about how to make him pay. I went back into the dressing room and changed into a fishnet body stocking and some black heels. I covered my face with a Mardi Gras mask, securing it with bobby pins to my pinned-up my hair.

I went back into the main club area and spotted my father

at a table with three dancers cooing and flirting with him. His tie was now hanging loosely from his neck and his top three buttons were open. I walked over to him slowly and stood directly in front of him with my back turned. I got some mean looks from the other dancers, but I didn't care. I just started swaying seductively in front of my father.

I could tell he was getting into it from the oohs and ahhs that were coming out of his sickening mouth. I turned around and made sure to keep my chin up so he couldn't see my eyes through the mask. I rubbed my breasts and moved my hand down to my crotch. Then he pulled out his wad and threw some bills toward me. There was about a thousand lying on the floor in front of me, but I still wasn't satisfied.

I turned back around and bent forward, showing the perfectly positioned opening in the crotch of my body stocking. This sent him over the edge, and soon, there was about five thousand dollars on the floor for me.

I turned around, began picking up the bills. Once I had them securely in my hand, I began to walk away. I removed my mask and said, "Thanks for the tips, Daddy."

The look on his face was priceless. He jumped up and moved toward me, but I motioned for Tre, the bouncer to cut him off. I looked back to make sure Tre had kept him at bay, and then I went back into the dressing room and laughed until I cried. All the while I was counting and re-counting the bills my father had put down.

Before closing time, I made sure to tell Tre not to let that man back in the club because he had been harassing me. I slipped him a thousand dollars and he smiled and nodded.

I went home that night and did some online shopping. I would call it a victory spree. I purchased a few thousand in shoes and handbags and went to bed with a smile on my face. I kept seeing my father's look of pure horror when I took the mask off. It made me smile. That was the moment I knew I wanted him dead. I didn't know how I would do it, but I knew he had to go.

I met Evan the following night. It was perfect. I knew he had to know some hit men from his time in jail. All I had to do was convince him that it was going to be worth his while.

Chapter 21

Lucas

I couldn't believe Raquelle actually helped us tear down the equipment after the show. She seemed like one of the guys, wrapping up mic cords, helping the drummer put his cymbals away, and ripping up the duct tape that held the equipment down. She even helped load some stuff into my van. I tried to offer her a cut of the gig money, but she wouldn't hear of it.

"Please, don't insult me. It was nothing." She let her long hair out of the bun and took a big gulp of the bottled water I had just handed her. It was a sight to behold.

"OK, then you at least have to let me take you to breakfast."

"Now that, I can get with." She placed her finger on her chin for a second. "But only if it's IHOP and I can get some Swedish pancakes."

"Deal. Give me a minute to give the guys their money and we're outta here."

We listened to Alicia Keys on the van ride to IHOP and

talked mostly about music. I asked her if she knew who Leela James was to see if my theory was correct.

"Of course. I have the CD, and it has a permanent residence in my changer at home. I like all the songs, but my favorites are 'Ghetto' and 'When You Love Someone'."

I just smiled.

Once we had had our fill of pancakes and all the fixings, we sipped decaf and talked. I told her all about Jay-Ron and the struggle I was having with him. I also told her how I was researching my family and had come up at a dead end.

"Don't feel bad. I don't even know my father's name."

"Seriously?"

"My mother told me I didn't want to know, that he was a bad man and she was protecting me from him. She died before I got a chance to really talk to her about it. All she told me was that he was still in Louisiana." She looked like she was in a daze for a second. "But anyway, keep looking. I'm sure you'll find something."

Raquelle also encouraged me to fight for Jay-Ron's future, but not to get myself killed in the process.

I think the waitress was ready for us to leave because she kept coming over and asking us if we needed anything else.

"Don't worry," she looked at the woman's name tag, "Marla." She handed the woman a twenty.

Marla looked at the twenty like it was a piece of a radioactive meteor.

"It's your tip," Raquelle explained.

Marla got a big smile on her face, sat the decaf pot on the table, and that was the last we saw of her. I was impressed by her generosity and a little mad that I hadn't thought of it first.

When our coffee had run out, we decided to leave. The

ride to her house was encased in an easy comfortable silence except for the music that was coming out of the speakers at a low volume.

She directed me to her house and I parked on the street in front of it.

"Can I walk you to the door?"

She tilted her head and smiled. "Of course."

She searched her bag for her keys and finally was able to unlock the door.

"Thanks for breakfast," she said.

"I should be the one thanking you for all the stuff you helped us pack up."

She let out a soft chuckle. "Please. It was my pleasure."

The lighting on her porch made her eyes sparkle, and the smell of sweet vanilla mixed with the remnants of pecan syrup drove me over the edge.

I wrapped my arms around her waist and pulled her in close to me.

"Raquelle—" I began.

"Shut up," she said, planting her soft lips on mine.

The kiss was sweet but erotic. I could feel my man coming to life in my jeans while I inhaled her breath.

After what seemed like ten seconds, but was probably closer to three minutes, she backed up and looked into my eyes. The moisture in her eyes told me what she didn't say. She took my hand and led me inside her home, which I was impressed with. It had a warm, inviting feeling to it, and it was just like I imagined it to be.

She closed and bolted the door, kicked off her shoes and came back over to where I stood in the middle of the living room. We kissed and held each other for a while, and then we moved to the sofa. I know we made out like teenagers for a few minutes before we came up for a breath.

She went over to the CD player and I heard Leela's voice come through the speakers. She came over and held out her hand to me.

We danced in a slow, rhythmic sway—the closeness not really sexual, but rather, more intimate. When the song was over, we sat back down and just looked at each other for a while.

"Raquelle, do you know I've had a thing for you since you and my sister became friends in high school?"

"No. I didn't. I had a crush on you since the day I was at your house going to the bathroom and you came out wearing nothing but a white, fluffy towel." She smiled and I took her hand.

"Seriously?"

"No lie."

She sighed and shifted a little.

"It's late, and as much as I want to take you in the bedroom and show you, I think it'd be best if we didn't," I said.

She pressed her lips together and nodded. I stood and pulled her up to me. We kissed again, and I was reassured by the same feelings rushing over me.

I took a deep breath and exhaled the words before I lost my nerve. "I don't want this to be the last time I taste your lips. I think I might be addicted."

She smiled. "It won't be," she said. A tiny drop of wetness ran about halfway down her cheek before losing its steam. I wiped it away and smiled.

"Good night, Raquelle."

"Good night, Lucas"

I drove home and sat in the van for about twenty minutes before I could bring myself to go in the house. I didn't want to go to sleep because that would mean the night was over.

I went inside and took a shower and got back on the computer. Raquelle's encouragement had inspired me to dig deeper to figure out what was behind all the mystery with my father. I thought about coming out and asking him or my mother about it. However, I knew that they were the type of people who didn't like to be questioned. If they wanted you to know something, they'd make sure you knew it.

Chapter 22

Layla

After the How To Please A Woman course let out, I lingered in the classroom for a while to speak with Marguerite about how things had gone. She was at the back of the room speaking with some of the students, so I just stood there and waited.

At first I didn't notice Sierra sitting there, but she cleared her throat to get my attention. I was a little uncomfortable, but walked over to where she sat. I still had a feeling she was a spy for Catalina.

"Hey, Sierra. How are you liking the workshops?"

I tried to be all businesslike, but I was squirming a little. "They're great. You really have something here. I think this is going to help a lot of people liberate themselves."

She glanced at the V my jacket made at the center of my chest. I smoothed my hands down the sides of my wide-leg trousers. "Glad to hear it." I turned to walk out of the class-room.

"Layla, wait." She stood up and landed about about six inches from my face. "Layla."

I looked into her eyes and breathed in the smell of her perfume. I could almost swear it was Amor Amor. She moved her hands to my waist and moved my glossy lips toward hers. My breathing labored, but then I remembered Marguerite and the others.

"I'm sorry," she said.

"No, don't apologize."

"Layla, I want to know you. Better." She moved closer once again, but I backed away.

"Sierra, look. I'm not sure I'm ready . . . I'm a little confused right now."

"It's okay. I understand." She picked up her Blackberry off the chaise and handed it to me. "Put your info in there. I'll email you so you'll have mine too. You can contact me first after that. It'll be up to you."

I hesitated and then started typing in the info. I handed it back to her and she grabbed her purse. Before she walked out, she said, "I really hope you'll get in touch."

I nodded and then moved to the tables where the students' empty refreshment cups sat.

Chapter 23

Raquelle

After teaching one of my popular Kama Sutra seminars, an attractive, thirty-something cocoa-colored lady wearing a pretty red peasant dress approached me as I was cleaning up the demonstration items.

She touched my shoulder with her manicured hand. "Raquelle, it was a *pleasure*." She smiled, showing her extra-white teeth.

"I'm glad you enjoyed it. I'm always hoping I'm able to teach the attendees a few new tricks." I winked and turned back to my lubricated mess.

"Oh, you did a great job." She moved a little closer and looked around the room. "Actually you did such a good job, I was wondering if you would be interested in holding a workshop for my circle of friends."

"Circle of friends?"

"We're swingers. We're already pretty sexually liberated," she giggled, "but everyone can stand to add a few new tricks to their bag."

"Oh."

She handed me a black, glossy card with a website address written on it. "The password is 'eatme.' Please, think about my proposition and contact me when you've reached a decision." With that, she sauntered out the door as Layla was coming in.

"What was that about?"

"Her name's Nina Baker. She wants me to hold a private seminar for her circle." I handed her the card. "You're coming with me."

"Okay."

She had no idea what she was getting herself into. I noticed then that there was something strange about the way she was acting. She was all fidgety and went around the room like a madwoman cleaning up the remnants of the class.

"You okay?" I asked.

She stopped for a second "Me? Oh yeah. I'm fine."

"You sure? How are things with Jabar?"

"Things are fine, but like I told you, I'm not looking for anything serious right now." She went back to straightening the room.

"Nothing serious, huh?"

"That's what I said."

"Now you know I know you better than that. If it ain't man trouble, what is it then?"

"It's nothing. Really. Now tell me about you and Lucas. Am I about to have a sister-in-law?"

I waved my hand. "We're just talking. That's all."

"Umph. It sounded like a lot more than that when he told me about you two at IHOP. I think if it wasn't open twenty-four hours, you two would have shut the place down."

I wiped some honey dust off the instructor table and on to the floor. "What did he say?"

"Wouldn't you like to know?"

"Heffa. What's with you and all the secrets today?"

"Nothing! OK, all he said was it was one of the best nights he's ever had."

"He said that?"

"Yep. What'd you do to him? Put a few of your advanced techniques on him?"

"No. It wasn't even like that. It wasn't even about sex. It was more like connection."

"I know what you mean."

I dropped a bottle of Oil of Love on the floor. "Fuck!" I picked the bottle up and examined it. "Thank God it didn't break."

"Have you ever thought about being with a woman?" Layla asked.

I looked at her like she asked me if I'd ever drunk milk directly from a cow. "What brought that on?"

"Nothing. I was just wondering."

"Well, I've never acted on anything, but research has shown that most women fantasize about sex with another woman. Why?"

"I saw Sierra."

My eyes got wide. "Sierra again?"

"Yeah, she's taking the How To Please A Woman class. Did you know?"

"No, since Marguerite is teaching that one."

"Right."

"So you kissed her?"

"Yeah. I'm kind of worried it'll get back to Lucas."

"You think? I'm pretty sure Lucas and Catalina don't talk anymore."

"Yeah, but I don't want that nutcase to have something on me." She turned to leave.

"Layla?"

"Yeah?"

"Don't be ashamed about exploring new things. We're human."

"I know."

"Okay, as long as you know."

Later that night, I had scheduled my three-week Intermediate Voyeurism course to go on a field trip to a club called Fishbowl. There were eight of us, including me, so we all carpooled to the location in the alleys of Foggy Bottom. There were three females, including myself, and five males. For the most part, they were all pretty quiet students thus far. Who knows? Maybe they were into watching me.

So we got to the Fishbowl and I explained the rules of engagement to them.

"OK, so you can look but not touch, unless they ask you to."

A few of the students gave me a weird look, but the majority of them were ready to let the games begin.

"Let's go to the bar before we start the circuit."

I had explained to them in last week's class that Fishbowl's basic concept was a long, winding hallway of rooms. There was glass that separated the employees from the customers, who could watch them perform different sex acts, both alone and with partners.

The basic rule was only to observe unless you were singled

out by one of the employees. At that point, you could choose to either engage in the activity or decline. My bet was most voyeurs would decline the invitation, preferring instead to simply watch from afar. I was planning on testing out that theory.

After we got out drinks, we began moving through the first wave of scenes. The first scene was a buff man with wooden clothespins attached to his nipples, neck, upper lip, foreskin, and ball sac.

The students looked both shocked and awed by that one. The man didn't point to any of us, so we moved on to the next window. Inside this room was an Asian lady riding a bucking bronco with a vibrating dildo sticking up off the seat. She wore a cowgirl hat and boots and nothing else. She saw us and pointed to Julio, one of my most vocal students. He wasn't too vocal at that moment, though. He shook his head and took off toward to next window. I shrugged at the lady and we all moved on.

By the time we had reached the last of the 28 rooms, my theory was proven every time except once. There was a room about halfway through where a sexy young blonde was wearing pigtails and pink pajamas and eating an ice cream cone. She pointed to Harold, an overweight thirty-something guy, to come join her and he did have a lick or two.

I was satisfied with the trip but totally exhausted once I made it home. I was too tired to do anything but take a quick shower and climb in my bed butt naked. I did wonder for a minute if there were any voyeurs watching me from across the street, but then I was asleep before I could ponder it too much.

Chapter 24

Lucas

"There has been a shooting this evening in Southeast Washington. A fourteen-year-old male was found wounded near the entrance of the Southeast Hospital."

I took another bite of my lo mein before it hit me. Then I pressed rewind on my DV-R and played it again. As soon as I heard fourteen-year-old male, my stomach flipped. For some reason, I knew it was Jay-Ron. I booked out the door without even grabbing a jacket.

I ran quite a few stoplights and pissed off some drivers on my way to the hospital. I approached the front desk of the emergency department and asked the receptionist, who was chatting on her cell phone, if she had any information on the condition of Jay-Ron Jenkins and if I could see him.

She popped her gum and rolled her eyes at me before telling the caller, "Hold on, Martina." She looked at me. "Are you the patient's immediate family?"

"No, I'm his teach—"

"I'm sorry, sir. I can't give out any patient information unless you're family. We have the Health Information Priv—"

"Well, can you verify that he's here? I'm the only family he
has."

She looked pissed that I had interrupted her as she
twisted her mouth up and started typing on the terminal.
"Yeah, he's here, but you ain't heard that from me. He's in
surgery right now. Go to the third floor and you'll see a waiting room there."

"Thanks."

"Umph." She rolled her eyes again and went back to her
cell phone.

I ran over to the elevator and pressed the button about
fifty times before the doors finally opened. I rode the short
ride up two levels. I found the waiting room and saw no one
except an old woman in a blue hospital gown sitting on a
gurney in the hallway. She looked lost and right at home at
the same time. Either no one had shown up for Jay-Ron, or
they were taking a break. I sat down on one of the orange
pleather chairs and hung my head. I kept thinking that if I
hadn't been such a punk, I could have prevented this. But I
was too scared to get my damn shoes dirty with the shit that
surrounded Jay-Ron's life.

"You know these clowns told me they ain't have room for
me?" the old woman said.

I looked over at her and she nodded her confirmation.

"Really?"

"Yes, sir. Told me they ain't have a room for me and rolled
my old behind out in the hallway. What are you doing around
these parts anyway? Looking like you just stepped outta *GQ*
magazine." She threw her head back and started laughing
and broke into a coughing/choking fit.

I went over to her and patted her on the back a few times.

"Thanks, baby. Whew, you just don't realize you getting old until it sneaks up on you one day and bites you in the ass." She cleared her throat and patted her chest. "Anyway, you ain't answer my question. What you doing looking like you lost?" She looked my khaki and Polo clad body up and down.

"I'm here for one of my students. He was shot this evening."

"Mmm." She pulled her flowered robe tighter around her neck. "Seems like they's a lot of that going 'round."

"What do you mean?"

"Seems like every day somebody else done got shot for one thing or another. You'd think the nation's capital would be the safest place in the country. Shoot, most people scared to go out they house after dark." She glanced at me. "Least in these parts. Can you get me a drink of water from the fountain?" She handed me a clear plastic cup that looked like it had seen better days.

I went over to the rusty, crusty fountain and filled her cup. "You sure you want to drink this?" I held the cup up to the light.

"What are my options? Drink that or go thirsty? Gimme that."

I handed her the cup. "Wait a minute." I went over to the vending machine and got a bottle of water and brought it to her.

"Thanks, baby. But I'll just take this here." She held the cup up before taking a sip from it.

"Why?"

"'Cause you ain't gonna be 'round forever. And sometimes it's better to get used to what you do have 'stead of all the time wanting something you ain't got."

I sat back down in my chair and tried to make sense of what she said, but it was no use. Thoughts of Jay-Ron flooded my head. I thought back to when the first day I taught him a private lesson. He had told me he couldn't afford private lessons, and would rather just stick with the group learning. I had told him the lessons were free, but he sort of brushed me off. It took about six weeks before I convinced him to meet me after school for the private lessons twice a week. He had reacted the same way when I took him food shopping.

Then it hit me. He was probably scared that I was only a temporary fixture, and so he didn't want to get his hopes up to have them crushed down the road.

I hung my head and covered my eyes. "You know, you're a very wise woman." I turned my body to where the woman had been, but she was gone.

I went outside and called Raquelle to tell her what had happened.

"I'll be right there," she said.

"You don't have to—"

"You heard me. Hang in there."

Within thirty minutes, she was walking out of the elevator. She came over and hugged me. It felt good to have her close to me. It was such a stark contrast to the way Catalina was. In a good way. The last week since our IHOP outing had been great. We either saw each other or talked every day. I was definitely falling for her, if I hadn't already.

"I'm so sorry, Lucas. Do you know anything yet?"

"Not yet. I've been waiting here for over an hour, and no one has come out yet."

We sat in the waiting room holding hands until an Indian man in scrubs came out and asked, "Jay-Ron Jenkins?"

I stood up. "Yes, we're here for him. I'm his—uh—brother."

"I'm Dr. Kitu. Mr. Jenkins needs a blood transfusion. I am going to need permission from his guardian."

I looked at Raquelle. She nodded. "I'm his guardian," I said.

"Fine, Mr . . . ?

"Lane. Lucas Lane."

"Okay, now to the bad news. Your brother lost a lot of blood, and like I said, he will need a transfusion. The problem is, the blood banks are low on his blood type. Since you are his brother, would you be willing to see if you are a match?"

I was afraid. I had just lied to this man about being Jay-Ron's brother, and now I was about to be exposed. I figured there was a chance I was a match, so I went for it.

"Sure, not a problem."

Raquelle gripped my hand.

"Okay then, Mr. Lane. Let's get you down to the lab."

He told us where the lab was, and Raquelle and I briefly stood outside the door before going in.

"You're so brave," she said.

"Not brave. Crazy . . . Maybe, but brave? No."

She gave me a quick kiss, and we went in the lab. Miraculously, it turned out I was a match. The blood donation process was grueling. I kept feeling like I was going to puke all over the place, but I closed my eyes and relived Jay-Ron's last concert, where he banged out a blues medley.

We went back up to the ICU waiting room and played the

waiting game again. I held Raquelle's hand while we watched the beaten up television. Dr. Kitu came back about an hour later and told us the transfusion was underway.

"Your brother will be fine. As soon as the transfusion is complete, we will remove the bullet. Thankfully, it didn't puncture any vital organs. He should be out of surgery in about an hour."

I breathed a sigh of relief, and Raquelle squeezed my hand.

After the doctor left, I said, "Can you believe that? A twenty percent chance of the blood type matching, and it matched."

"Actually, it's probably less than that. I think AB is one of the rarest types."

"Wow."

"Someone was looking out for Jay-Ron."

"Isn't that the truth?"

She rubbed the top of my back. "What you did was really admirable."

"I guess I felt like I owed him. I still don't know why he was shot. I hope it wasn't because of me." I kept thinking about Ace and the fight at the apartment.

We went and got some chips and sodas from the snack machines and resumed our perch in the waiting room. A few hours later, Dr. Kitu came out and told us that the surgery had gone as planned and that Jay-Ron would be unconscious for a while. He told us to go home and get some rest and that we could come back in the morning.

Raquelle came back to my place. I gave her a T-shirt to put on, and we laid in each other's arms until sunrise. While I laid there, something earth shattering happened. It all came together at that moment.

Yasmeen Jenkins. Jay-Ron Jenkins. Ancestry. The website. My father.

"Holy shit!"

Raquelle jumped up. "Who's there?"

"Sorry, sweetie. Go back to sleep. I think I just figured out why me and Jay-Ron have the same blood type."

Chapter 25

Layla

Raquelle called and told me what happened with Jay-Ron, and that she'd be with Lucas for the day. We cancelled her classes and I sat in on Marguerite's Bondage Techniques class, which was the only one scheduled for that day.

I was surprised by the variety of people interested in bondage. I guess I had always been a little reserved on the sexual front, but it fascinated me to know that so many people were living their sex lives up. I wanted a piece of that action. I felt I had been too good for too long and it had gotten me nowhere.

After the class let out and Marguerite and I cleaned up, I sat in my car thinking. The thought came to me that it would be a good day to straighten out the Sierra thing.

I went home and got on the computer after fixing myself a late lunch. Her email was sitting in my inbox just like she said. I replied, telling her that I thought we should have a talk. I gave her my phone number and told her to call me if she got a free moment.

The phone rang about an hour later. She told me it was her day off and then gave me directions to her place. I thought it would be better to have the talk face to face. Plus, there was a part of me that wanted something to happen between us. I wanted to see her in person so I could tell if it was a fantasy I wanted to live out, or if I would chicken out when push came to shove. I wanted to go to her house rather than have her come to me, so I could bolt if I needed to.

She opened the door for me, looking cute in her short, yellow athletic-inspired dress and matching sneakers. Her smile was welcoming.

"Can I get you something to drink? Lemonade? Soda? Wine? Hypnotic?"

I didn't want any alcohol clouding my judgment. So I went with the lemonade. As I sat on a chaise in her living room, I remembered Catalina.

She came out and handed me the glass of lemonade.

"Sierra, I have to ask you something."

She sat adjacent to me on the sofa. "Sure."

"I just want you to know that whatever goes on between us stays between us. This is sort of a confusing time for me, and I really don't want certain things getting back to my brother."

She smiled. "If you're worried about me gossiping to Catalina, you can stop. She and I are kind of on the outs. I actually haven't spoken to her in forever. I told you that at the grand opening."

"Oh, I guess I'm just paranoid."

"OK, my turn to ask you something."

"OK."

"Have you ever kissed a woman before? Don't get me wrong. When we kissed at the party, it was spectacular. I just got the feeling that it was something new to you."

I took a long drink of my lemonade. "No, I've never kissed a woman, and yes, it was new."

She nodded once. "So, I guess that answers my next question."

"Which was?"

"Have you ever been intimate with a woman?"

"Other than myself, no." A nervous smile adorned my face.

She laughed. "Well, that's better than some women can say. But I'm sure the illustrious Raquelle keeps you informed about all that."

"Yeah, she's always giving me tidbits." My eyes got wide. "Wait, that didn't come out quite right."

We both laughed until tears were forming in the corners of my eyes. It was so hard for me to believe that someone as cool as Sierra would hang out with Crazy Catalina.

She came over and sat next to me on the edge of the chaise. Her legs looked so soft and shiny, I wanted to touch them. They were slightly parted, and the yellow terry fabric was pulled taut around them.

She must have noticed me looking because she moved her hand down to brush against them. This made it easy for her to move to my feet. She pulled off my shoe and softly touched the sole of my foot. A shiver ran up through my legs, landing right between them. I glanced at her face for a moment, and she was looking directly at me. I returned my gaze to my leg when her soft fingers slowly crawled from my ankle, to my calf, and to my knee. She stopped there, looking at my face to see my reaction, but I said nothing. She took the silence for agreement and continued her climb to my thigh. I thanked God that I had decided to wear a skirt.

She repositioned herself to face me, and I could see that she had no panties on. It was like the scene from *Basic*

Instinct when Sharon Stone revealed her bare crotch to the interrogators. Except in this case, I knew I could have it if I wanted it, and it was then that I knew I wanted to step outside myself and experience something new. Something sexual. Something pleasurable.

Her kisses were feather light at first, moving from the tip of my toes to mid-thigh, where my skirt ended. When she reached that point, she looked up at me as if to get my permission to continue. My response was to bite my lip, and then I leaned forward to kiss her on the mouth. I took her hand and placed it on my skirt, telling her I wanted her to continue. She made her way to my black lace, and her fingers softly stroked the front of them while our lips continued to dance.

She stood up and took off her dress, shoes, and socks. She wore some cute little white thongs with yellow flowers and nothing else. Looking at her standing in front of me naked made me bolder, and I unbuttoned my shirt and tossed it aside. I got up and removed my skirt and bra. We stood there in front of each other, drinking each other in until we couldn't take it any longer.

"Follow me," she said, walking toward the back of the house. We entered her bedroom, which was done all in white and dark wood. A painting of a calla lily was the only thing that adorned her white walls.

"Make yourself comfortable," she told me as she motioned toward the bed.

She walked to the dark mahogany dresser and opened one of the top drawers. She glanced back at me through the mirror and I rested my black lace behind on her soft white comforter.

She joined me on the bed with a red velvet bag in her

hand. She took all five of the fluffy white bed pillows and stacked them in front of one another.

"Lean back there and just relax."

My heart was racing. I couldn't believe I was about to be sexed by another woman. Two voices in my head competed for my attention. One said, "Run" and the other said, "Fuck it."

I listened to the latter and rested back on the pillows and closed my eyes. Sierra pulled some chocolate scented body butter from her bag and warmed a dollop between her fingers. She started massaging my breasts, moving in a slow, circular motion and adding surprising but gentle twists of my nipples. Electric shockwaves coursed through my veins. I was starting to ache between my legs and I couldn't control the moan of pleasure that escaped my lips.

She continued her massage down to the waistband of my low-cut panties, pressing gently on the area above my pubic mound. My legs involuntarily spread and I opened my eyes to see a smile spread across her face.

"Layla, you're so beautiful." She pulled on the waistband of my panties and I lifted my bottom up so she could remove them the rest of the way.

She leaned forward between my legs and planted a soft kiss on my lips before diving between my legs. I felt her soft fingers part my lips and I looked down to see her admiring my view. The anticipation was killing me, but I still had that voice inside my head telling me to run. It was silenced as soon as she put her mouth on me and softly and rhythmically licked my clitoris.

She placed one hand under my ass and tickled my opening with the other. I could feel the pressure mounting as she continued the pulsating tongue job, and when she placed one finger inside me and slowly thrust it in and out of me, I saw stars as my climax boiled over. It was the most intense and powerful orgasm I had ever experienced.

I laid there for a minute without saying anything. There were a million thoughts running through my head, but the one that stood out was, "Damn."

I felt her crawl up close to me and rest her head on my stomach. I wasn't sure what I was supposed to do. I wasn't versed on the lesbian thing, so I didn't know if it was my turn to reciprocate or what.

It almost seemed like she read my mind when she said, "Don't worry. I just want to lie here with you."

I breathed an internal sigh of relief and removed two of the pillows from behind me to place on the other side of the bed for her. Then I leaned back and drifted into a sweet, but tormented slumber.

I heard my phone make the double chirp sound that let me know I had an incoming text message. After I confirmed that Sierra was dozing, I quietly got up and went to check the phone. It was a message from Jabar asking me if I was free for dinner and a movie.

I went to the bathroom and found Sierra awake when I returned.

"I need to go."

She looked disappointed, but nodded and walked me to the door. My legs were still a little rubbery, but somehow I was able to walk to the car. I looked back and saw Sierra standing in the window with a sad expression.

I sighed and texted Jabar back to let him know I was free for the evening. I was tired, but I also felt guilty. I felt like I needed to make it up to him even though he had no idea that there had been a woman between my thighs.

I went home, showered, and dressed for the date with Jabar. I kept seeing his handsome face and Sierra's naked breasts in flashes. It was wearing me out.

Amid all the confusion, there was one thing I knew for certain. I was going to have to commend Marguerite on the How To Please A Woman seminar. It looked like at least one of her students was taking notes.

Chapter 26

Evan

Kitty called me a couple weeks after our night at the
Doubletree and asked if we could meet up to discuss
our business proposition. I had been going over the whole
idea in my head since then, and it was too big of an opportunity to pass up. I really ain't have anybody I could go to
and ask them to put out a hit on some folks, except this dud
Ace who I met in holding at the PG County jail. He told me
to look for him at Green Bay projects in Southeast if I ever
needed to eliminate somebody. I figured if I decided to go
ahead with it, he'd be the go-to guy.

Anyway, I didn't really trust the Kitty broad. I didn't know
much about her family, but from what I found out online,
they ain't seem that bad. Her mother was a dance teacher
who had her own studio, and she almost had her daughter
beat in the looks department. Her father was some fancy
lawyer.

I agreed to meet up with her at the Doubletree again, but
that was just because I knew my phone was probably tapped

or some shit, so I wasn't about to say anything incriminating over the phone. Plus, I thought there might be some way I could get some money out of her.

I was laying back in the hotel room, watching an old *Saturday Night Live* rerun when I heard a light tap on the door. I let her in and she was all business. She pulled a manila envelope out of her bag and handed it to me.

"All the information your associate will need is in there; his routine, pictures, everything." She took a seat at the desk.

I sat down on the bed facing her and put the folder aside. "There's something else I need to know. Why are you doing this?"

"You aren't being paid to know why. You just need to carry out your end of the deal, and I promise you, you won't ever have to work again."

There was an evil look in her eyes. I had seen some cold-blooded folks up in prison, but there was something in her eyes even they didn't have. Maybe it was because they had been beat down by the system, but she had a gleam of determination that I hadn't seen in any of them.

"Well, I ain't gonna be a part of killing innocent people, so you better convince me that he deserve what about to get."

She rolled her eyes. "I don't like being questioned like this, but since I need your help, I'll tell you. He cut me off and is forcing me to pay my medical bills."

She acted like she had just said they had molested her or beat her on a daily. This broad was definitely lunchin'.

"I don't know about where you come from, but murder is a life in prison type of crime. Whether it's hired or done by your own hands," I told her.

"Don't fuck it up and it'll be fine. If you fuck this up though, you will be going down with me."

I was still feeling shook, but I didn't want her to catch on to that. "This is your father, though, shorty. Isn't there any other way to get money?"

"There was, until that bitch ruined my plans." Her back was bone-straight now. "I was going to marry the money, but that bitch came in and took my man."

She seemed a lot more heated about this chick, and I at least felt like the girl wasn't innocent like the father. She had, after all, came in and stolen someone's man.

"Well, why don't you get her out of the way first? See if that will solve your problem?"

An evil, Grinch-like smile came across her face. "No. But I do appreciate the thought."

"Aight, I'll do this, but my man is going to need to know what you know about your father, his habits, whatever."

"Most of it's in the folder. If you need anything further, you can contact me."

"Okay then."

She stood up and moved toward the door. "In the meantime, you just secure the labor."

"No problem."

"OK, then. Expect a call from me in a couple of days."

I just nodded and closed the door behind her. I sat down on the bed with my head in my hands trying to figure out what the fuck just happened. I was still blown that I had just agreed to broker a murder for hire.

I laid back on the bed and stared at the ceiling, trying to figure out my next move. I knew I needed to get up with Ace, but my mind just kept drifting.

The Catalina bitch was like a spoiled baby throwing a tantrum. I hated people like that—people who thought their problems were so serious, when they had it better than ninety percent of America.

Ace probably wouldn't be out and about until after midnight, so I decided to take advantage of the room and take a nap for a few. I woke up around eleven and jumped in the shower before heading out and dropping the room key off at the front desk. The drive from Pentagon City to Green Bay wasn't that long, so I ain't really have time to stop and think enough to kirk myself out. The more I thought about the whole thing, the less I wanted to go through with that shit, so it was best for me to just get it over with quick as possible.

I rolled up into Green Bay and there was a rack of folks standing out in front of the entrance, in the parking lot, and in the lawns. I rolled through the lot once to see if I could see Ace, but he wasn't out there. I pulled up beside a cute shorty wearing the hell out of some jeans.

"Ay, shorty. You know where I can find Ace at?"

She walked up beside my car and leaned down to get a better look at me. "Who you?"

"I was locked up with him a while back. He told me I could find him out here if I ever needed to contact him."

She looked at me for a minute and then said, "He'll be back in a few. He went down to the carry out to get something to eat."

"Aight then." I backed into a parking spot that gave me a good look at the cars coming in the lot. I didn't have to wait long before a white Ford Excursion pulled in the lot and Ace got out carrying white bag in one hand and his celly in the other. He leaned up against the car and yelled into his phone. He was wearing a white rag on his head, a white hoodie, and some fresh white Nikes.

I got out the car and approached him slow, but not too slow. I ain't want him to think I was 'bout to run up on him.

"Ay, man."

He recognized me. He smiled, held up his pointing finger, and then went back to cursing out the person on the other end of the phone.

"Ma'fucka, I told your ass already. I want my fuckin' money. It's real simple. You either bring me my shit or bring me my money. Don't make me tell you again, young." He clicked off the phone and put it back in the holster on his belt.

"Ma'fuckin' EV. What the fuck you been up to, boy?" We exchanged pounds.

"Just got out a minute ago. Got a business prop for ya."

"Aight, aight. Get in the car, man. I don't trust none of these folks out here."

I got in the passenger side of the Excursion and he got back in the driver's seat.

"Ay, man. You want a wing or some shit?" He held up the white Styrofoam container.

"Nah, man. I'm good."

"So what you got for me, young?" He opened the container and started fixing up his food.

"Check it out. I met this honey at the strip club who needs some professional work done. She's paying top dollar. $500 gees."

He just about spilled his mumbo sauce all over his white. "No fuckin' shit?"

"Nah, man. She some high society ho that wants her pops to get gone."

"No shit. Rich folks. What the fuck is wrong with 'em?"

"I don't know, man. Anyway, you game?"

"Fuck yeah, I'm game. But check it out, man. I want 15% of the fee up front. I ain't fucking around with these rich people. I done got burned by they asses before."

Chapter 27

Raquelle

For some reason, I pictured the Elite Circle to look like a bunch of people you wouldn't want to see naked. I was pleasantly surprised when we walked into the large den at Nina Baker's house. All the people there were almost as beautiful as she was. It was like a gathering of retired models or something. No one had an extra roll. No one had a scuff on their shoe. No one was anything less than perfection.

The men ranged in age from fairly young bucks to distinguished looking gentlemen. None of the women looked to be a day over forty, but I had learned that there were plenty of tricks for fooling Mother Nature if you had the cash and a good doctor.

Layla and I followed Nina to the lower level of the house, where we would be giving our workshop.

"I think we'll be comfortable down here," Nina said.

There was a huge room down there with large sofas, chaise lounges, and soft, velvety carpet. There was a large circular table in the center of the room and I took my bag over there to unpack my materials. I was to teach the same Kama Sutra class Nina had been a part of, so I had my honey dust, feather teaser, and other supplies ready to go.

Nina went back upstairs and Layla took a seat on one of the chaises. She looked a little uncomfortable.

"You OK over there?"

She snapped out of what seemed to be a temporary trance. "Yeah, I was just thinking how different this was from what I expected."

"I feel you."

About thirty minutes later, the guests began tricking into the lower level, taking seats around the room. I couldn't really tell who were couples, as they all just seemed to interact evenly together. It was a strange situation, but I had studied these things, and I was as ready as I could possibly be.

After everyone had settled in, I began my lecture with a brief history of Kama Sutra and moved into some of the basic level massage and foreplay techniques.

I used willing volunteers to demonstrate the positions. A pretty light-skinned girl named Teena and a muscular, chocolate brother named Phillip were chosen to demonstrate the positions. They all got naked and into it pretty quickly. I showed them how to position themselves in everything from The Rider to the more complicated Pillar, where both the man and woman are kneeling. They were able to do most of the positions with my instruction.

After the position demo, I looked around the room to better gauge where the rest of the Circle were at mentally. They all had lustful looks in their eyes, including Layla, who repeatedly crossed and uncrossed her legs.

Nina stood and approached me. "Great job. You've got them all hot and panting."

I smiled.

"Will you and your associate stay and partake?"

"No, but we can stay and observe for a while if that's OK."

"Perfectly fine."

I motioned for Layla to come help me put my materials away. We turned our backs for a moment to pack up and within a few moments, we heard moaning and groaning around us.

Someone had pulled out a few sex chairs and a Monkey Rocker, and they were already occupied by the swingers. I pulled Layla to an empty section of the sofa and we sat down.

"Watch and learn, my dear."

"This is crazy." She huffed and crossed her legs.

"Don't be afraid to learn something new."

She just rolled her eyes at me.

My eyes became glued to a foursome on the floor in front of me. One woman was riding another woman's face while she orally pleased a man. The first woman was getting pounded by a second man.

I glanced at Layla to see if she was still mentally with me, and I saw her eyes get wide as the face rider stood and bent forward in front of the man she was orally pleasing. He squirted some lube on her ass and entered her rectum. The other guy came and stood behind him, and within a few minutes they rotated. The other woman was providing oral intermission for the waiting man.

Layla looked at me with the look of death and I decided I had better get her out of there before she killed me. I went over to Nina, who was leaning back on a chaise having her pussy eaten by a young buck.

"Thanks, Nina. We're going to go."

"No, thank you. Your check's in the mail." She winked and then went back to her activity.

When we got to the car I spoke first. "I thought it was exciting, erotic, and educational."

Layla just looked at me and rolled her eyes before pulling out of out parking spot on the quiet suburban street.

Chapter 28

Catalina

"Seventy-five thousand? You idiot, if I had that kind of cash lying around, why would I need to get my inheritance early?" I couldn't believe that thuggish asshole could be so stupid.

"Look, I'm just telling you what he said."

"Will he take a smaller deposit? I have about 20K."

"Nah. He wants 75 or nothing."

I started going through all my investments, real estate, and other assets in my head. I could probably sell some of it off, but I needed him to complete the job sooner rather than later, and everyone knows selling investments isn't a five minute thing.

"I need some time to get the cash together for the retainer, but you will have your million as soon as my father's estate is doled out."

"Hey, I understand all of that, but my man is a professional, and just like your Daddy's law firm, he don't do no jobs without seeing the money first."

"Please. Will you just talk to him? I'm going to need about

ten business days to come up with the retainer, but my mother's going out of town tomorrow and won't be back for three days. He'll be at the house alone."

"I'll try, but I don't think it'll happen." He got up from the bench and made his way to his car.

I had to figure out a way to get this all to go off without a hitch before my mother came back from out of town. Yes, she was in cahoots with my father on this money thing, but she was still fairly innocent, as opposed to him.

My father had someone spy on me at Chica's. Tre told me he had seen the man, who was watching me entirely too intently, come in the club with the man I had paid him to keep out. I had to give him even more money to throw that guy out and keep him out.

My father might have been a powerful attorney, but he didn't have the balls to come to my apartment to confront me. He had to know that he was wrong for putting me in this situation. He'd know exactly how wrong if I could get Thug Boy's jail buddy to do the damn job.

In the meantime, I called my broker to see if he could liquidate a few things and get me some cash.

"I'm sorry, Miss Richards. Your father has frozen all of your investment accounts. I'm afraid there's nothing I can do until he lifts the freeze."

"But those are my accounts. How can he have the power to do that?"

"He opened the accounts, and so his name was on each of them as a joint account holder."

I was enraged that my father had taken yet another step toward disinheriting me. And behind my back, no less. He had also just taken another step toward his own grave, and I would have to be sure he was pushed in head first before he had a chance to completely disinherit me.

Chapter 29

Lucas

I told Raquelle what I suspected when she came over after a private workshop. She had a giddy demeanor when she came in and flopped down on the sofa. I sat down beside her and told her what I had deduced.

"You know how I told you I didn't know much about my father's family?"

"Yeah."

"Well, I think I know why. He didn't want anyone to know."

"What do you mean?"

"I went to the library and looked at some old yearbooks from Jefferson High School. He was in there."

"Jefferson? Isn't that in—"

"Southeast. Yep."

"Well, maybe he was just trying to forget the struggle."

"Maybe, but that isn't the only thing I found. Yasmeen Jenkins also went there. And there was a photo of the prom where she and my father were posing for 'Most Likely To Get Married.'"

"Wait. Jenkins. You mean like Jay-Ron Jenkins?"

I nodded. "Yep."

"So what are you saying?"

I went to the computer desk and got the printout I had gotten from ancestry.com and handed it to her. "They were married."

She looked over the document and said, "Wow. This is deep. So you're saying Nikki and Jay-Ron are your brother and sister?"

"I can't say for sure, but it sure does look that way. With this stuff, the blood type match, and the connection I feel to the kid, I wouldn't doubt it."

She furrowed her brow. "Wait. This marriage license says they were married in 1974. When did he marry your mother?"

"A year before I was born. 1975."

"Did you find any divorce records?"

"Not yet. I'm going to see Jay-Ron in the morning and then go to the archives to see what I can find. There are basically two ways this could have played out. Either he never divorced Yasmeen and the marriage between he and my mother was illegal, or he divorced Yasmeen but continued to carry on a relationship with her."

I sat down beside her and leaned my head back. There were so many questions floating in my head, the primary one being "Who is my father?" It was like I had lived for thirty-one years as his son and never really knew him.

Raquelle rested her head on my chest and I wrapped my arms around her.

"I'll help you figure this out. I know what it's like to wonder about your father."

* * *

Jay-Ron looked small when I entered the hospital room late the next morning. I asked the middle-aged nurse who was bringing his lunch if anyone else had been to see him.

"No, you're the first."

She stood next to his bed and gently roused him from his sleep. "Wake up, baby. I have your lunch here."

Jay-Ron lifted his lids slowly, and when he saw me, they opened wide. "Mr. Lane, what are you doing here?"

The nurse raised her eyebrow at me.

"You know I'd be here to see how my *little brother* was doing." I winked at Jay-Ron.

"Oh, right."

The nurse grunted and shook her head before exiting the room.

I sat down in the visitor chair next to the bed. "I had to say I was your brother before they'd let me in."

"Yeah, the doctor told me I was alive because my brother donated blood for me to have a transfusion. I thought he was trying to talk hood speak." He smiled. "Thanks for doing that."

"Anytime." I tried to figure out where to start. "Do you remember what happened?"

"Yeah, I remember, but I ain't a snitch. The police were already here this morning trying to get me to give it up."

"Well, whatever we talk about stays between us."

He closed his eyes for a moment, seeming to mull over whether he should tell me.

"Ace hit Nikki because he thought she was flirting with another dude. I saw it happen, and I threatened him. He pulled a gun out, and that's all I remember. I don't even know how I got here."

I sat in silence for a minute, imagining what I would have

done if something similar had happened with Layla. "What you did was honorable, but you could've gotten yourself killed. I understand though. I probably would have defended my sister the same way."

He nodded and closed his eyes again.

"Jay?"

"Yeah?"

"What do you know about your father?"

"Why you asking me that for?"

"I was just curious to know what all you knew about him."

He was quiet for a while, looking over at me periodically. Finally, he said, "Not much, really. All I know is from what my mother and Nikki have told me. But I ain't asked in a while, ya know?"

I nodded.

"Ma used to call him Kel. She'd always talk about how great it would be when he came for us all—how we would be rich and not have to live in the hood anymore."

"Kel?"

"Yeah, like Keenan and Kel. Anyway, I was about ten when he stopped coming around."

"How old was your sister?"

"Eighteen, I guess."

"Okay."

"Well, Mama stopped talking about Kel. When I would ask her things, she'd get real sad and start crying. I didn't want her to cry, so I stopped asking. She died about two months after that. Then it was just me and Nikki. I think I was waiting for this Kel guy to come and bring us to live with him after Mama died, but he never came."

"What did you do after your mother died? Did child services come?"

"Nah, they don't really care about a couple of ghetto kids. My sister was a legal adult, so they just let us stay there by ourselves. We were doing okay with money because Nikki said Mama had a life insurance policy. But it ran out a couple of years later, and that's when she started being a gold digger."

"Ace?"

"Yeah, but there were others before him. They was cool with me being around, but Ace told her he wasn't trying to be no daddy. That was when she moved out and left me by myself. She brought money sometimes, but I mostly had to look out for self. You know the rest."

I nodded and looked at the tray of mystery meat covered in yellow gravy the nurse had left. "You want me to go get you some real food?"

"Yeah, man. I know beggars can't be choosers, but I don't think I can eat that." He grinned.

I went to Subway and brought him back a meal. I told him to get some rest and I would check on him later, and I headed for the archives to figure out the rest of the mystery surrounding my father and Yasmeen Jenkins.

Chapter 30

Layla

I kept replaying the night at Elite Circle over and over in my head. I was a little embarrassed by it, but I kept thinking about what Raquelle and I talked about on the way back from there.

I couldn't look at Raquelle on the way home from Nina's swinging extravaganza. I was embarrassed by what had just taken place. She didn't say anything for a while, but after about ten minutes, she started giggling softly. The giggle turned into a heartier laugh, and that turned into a laughing fit so bad she had to pull over.

"What's so funny, Raquelle?"

She wiped a tear from her eye. "Oh my God, girl. If you could have seen the look on your face when that woman took both of those dicks in her ass."

"Not funny."

"Oh, loosen up. That's probably going to be the highlight of your sex life."

She was probably right. I never thought I, the financial expert from the right schools and the right family would have ever been involved in something as freaky as being a voyeur at a swing party. But I had to admit, I liked it, and I wasn't totally opposed to the idea of something like it happening again, just as I wanted to have another experience with Sierra.

I just didn't know what to do about Jabar. I really liked him, but I was having thoughts about Sierra and the sex. We never did anything that night after watching the freaky DVD, but it was deeper than sex with him. We had a real connection. I was starting to wonder if I was squandering my one big chance at real love for really hot sex.

We had been texting back and forth, but it had been a couple of days since I had heard from Sierra. So I decided to get ready and surprise her.

After my shower, I sprayed a quick mist of Sweet Spot between my legs. I loved the smell of the stuff, and thought Sierra would appreciate it. I quickly dressed, in a skirt, of course, and headed to Sierra's place.

I hated just showing up on her doorstep, but I hadn't been able to get her out of my mind. Even when I spent time with Jabar, I would have flashbacks of the Elite Circle episode and the tryst with Sierra. I wanted to ask Raquelle if what I was feeling was normal, but she and Lucas were finally getting to enjoy each other, and I didn't want to stand in the way of that. They both deserved it.

Sierra opened the door looking surprised to see me. "Layla?"

"Were you expecting someone else?" I asked.

She stood there in her short teal terrycloth robe and looked over her shoulder. "Umm, no."

"Well, aren't you going to ask me in?"

"Who is it, sweetie?"

The voice that wafted out the door sounded strangely familiar, and I stood on my toes to try to see over Sierra's shoulder. She continued to stand there, wide-eyed and silent. Then, a face that had been infecting my memory appeared behind Sierra.

"Nina?"

Her full lips formed a smile. "Sierra, ask Miss Layla in."

Sierra was shocked by the exchange, but backed up to let me in. "You two know each other?"

Nina winked at me. She looked so pretty in her silky red robe. The color brought out the warm undertones in her skin—which I had seen a lot of that night at the private seminar.

"We've met each other in passing. I was attending a course at the school where Layla works," Nina explained.

I sighed my relief that she didn't go into details about the Elite Circle thing. I kind of wanted to get the hell out of there, but I couldn't. There were just too many possibilities. I was caught up like R. Kelly. My mind was telling me no . . .

"Drop your robe please, Sierra."

It was like Nina was calling the shots. Sierra looked at me and then let her robe fall to the floor as requested.

"Layla, I would love it if you would join us." Nina took Sierra's hand and pulled her in front of her. Her mouth was nearly exactly across from Sierra's pretty pussy.

Sierra looked a little pissed at first, but her demeanor changed when Nina buried her head between her legs. She propped her leg beside Nina on the chaise, allowing for easier access.

Nina paused from her lady lunch for a moment and slightly nodded her head for me to come join them.

"Sierra, dear. Help your friend undress," Nina said before going back to intermittently fondling and licking between Sierra's lips.

Sierra turned to me and pulled my dress over my head. I had taken the risk of wearing nothing under it, so I stood there totally bare.

Nina gazed from my toes to my calves. Then she moved up to my thighs, my pussy, and my navel. Her eyes roamed across my breasts to my collarbone to my lips. Finally, her gaze ended with my eyes.

I wasn't sure which of the beautiful ladies to look at, so I alternated, shifting my glances from Sierra's nakedness to Nina's silky passion and back again.

Nina motioned me to have a seat beside her. "Layla, have you ever given head to a woman?"

"No. No I haven't."

"Don't worry. It's simple. Do me a favor and close your eyes and lean back. Then, I want you to think about the best head you've ever received. Do you have it?"

I opened my eyes to look at Sierra before closing them again and saying, "Yes." I imagined our previous encounter and how perfect her technique was.

"Good. Now all you have to do is mimic those motions, those rhythms. We all like different things, but starting with what you like is a good place."

I opened my eyes and nodded.

"Let's try something brand new. Shall we?"

I was juicy by then, reliving the experience with Sierra, Nina's sexy voice, and Sierra's naked beauty. Nina moved to the soft ivory carpet and lay down on her back.

"Come here, Layla. I want you to sit on my face."

I hesitated for a second, but it seemed harmless enough,

so I knelt over her face and slowly lowered myself down. I felt a quick tongue stroke run from my clit to my opening.

"Mmm, Layla, you have a sweet pussy like Sierra."

Sierra didn't look at me, nor did she wait for any instructions from Nina. She got up and retrieved a strap-on that was hidden under one of the cushions on a chair and harnessed herself in. It was so erotic to see such a girly woman with a big dick hanging between her legs.

She positioned herself between Nina's legs, which were no spread nearly ninety degree angles. Sierra and I synced up our rhythms, looking each other in the eyes the entire time. I started bucking wildly and Nina grabbed me around the waist, pulling me down on her face. Sierra pumped her and played with her spot until I felt Nina's mouth vibrating against my orgasm-sensitive area, and there nothing I could do to keep from screaming. I rolled off of Nina's face and she lay there in an ecstatic trance. Sierra was left out yet again. I wondered if she enjoyed being the one to give the pleasure most of the time.

After a few minutes, Nina pulled herself from the floor and grabbed her clothing, and headed down the hall to the bathroom.

While Nina was in there, Sierra and I just lay there in silence. I still couldn't figure out why she seemed so pissed. It wasn't like she was interested in me or anything, right? It was just sex, right?

Nina exited the bathroom fully dressed in a white shift dress and black heels with white polka dots. "Ladies, thank you for a steamy afternoon. We really are going to have to do this again some time." She focused on Sierra. "I'll be in touch."

Sierra didn't respond.

Nina let herself out, and I moved to the bathroom. When I came out, Sierra was standing in her robe with her arms crossed.

"I have to—"

"Go. Yeah, I know." Her tone was sarcastic and a little insolent.

I guess she was getting used to the idea that I was coming over just for sex. I was thinking how I had become no better than a player who hits it then quits it.

"Right," I said. I pulled my jacket on and pulled my keys out of the pocket. "I'll call you."

"Whatever." She turned and went back into the bedroom.

When I got out to my car, I looked up at the window where Sierra had stood looking sad at me when I left the last time. This time, the window was empty.

Freak in the Sheets was alive with activity later that evening. Raquelle was holding a special speed dating activity, and close to a hundred people had signed up. We held the event in the main lounge area, and each woman sat at a table with a number. They would speak to each man, who wore a small numbered pin, for five minutes, and then, if they were interested in each other, they would write down the number on a sheet of paper they'd been given.

The event was a huge success, and as Raquelle and the other staff were cleaning up, I was doing a quick rundown of the books. Things were definitely looking good for us financially.

"Heya, are we rolling in the dough?" Raquelle bounced into my office and flopped down on the chair in front of my desk.

"We're doing all right." I smiled. "How's Jay-Ron doing?"

"I don't know everything, but Lucas thinks he may be your little brother."

"My what?" Damn. Had I been that out of the loop?

"Yeah, I'll let him fill you in on the details, but it looks like your father may have a checkered past."

I knew my parents didn't have the best relationship, but I never imagined my father had other children walking around. "You've got to be kidding me."

"Don't quote me on it, though. Like I said, he's looking into some things."

We wrapped up and walked out to our cars. I knew I needed to talk to my brother as soon as possible, so I called him on my way home.

"What the hell is going on? Raquelle just told me your student is our brother."

"Dag, sis. Quit screaming in my ear."

"Lucas Leonard Lane, if you don't tell me—"

"Yeah, yeah, I was going to tell you, but I wanted to get all the facts straight first."

"Well tell me now," I yelled.

"All right, jeez. Basically, the reason we never knew anything about Dad's past is because he didn't want us to know. He's from the ghetto. My guess is that Mother's parents wouldn't have approved of him, so he hid it."

"Okay, what about the kid?"

"I was getting to that. It looks like Dad was actually married to Jay-Ron's mother, Yasmeen Jenkins. He divorced her after he met Mother, but he kept a relationship with her and she had two kids, Nikki and Jay-Ron. So basically, they're our half-brother and half-sister."

"How did you figure all this out?"

"It was a number of things. I was researching Dad's side of the family, but kept hitting a brick wall. Actually, I saw the name Yasmeen Jenkins Lane, but figured it had to be another Kelvin Lane."

"Okay, so you were in denial."

"Basically. I mean, it just seems like we've been living a lie our whole lives."

"I wonder if Mother knows."

"That's my next step. I'm going to take Jay-Ron to meet them and see if she knows him. I'm going to try to get Nikki to come too, but she's been missing since the night Jay-Ron got shot."

"What about the mother, Yasmeen?"

"She died about seven years ago. Jay-Ron said he doesn't know how, but she got sick and passed."

"Wow."

"My thoughts exactly. I feel like if Jay-Ron is our brother, he deserves the same things we were given growing up. The problem is Mother."

"You can say that again. I'm pretty sure she's not going to be happy about all this."

"I'm not happy about it either. I just feel like I have to do what's right this time."

"Well, I'll come with you when you go."

"I appreciate that. Raquelle said she'll come along as well. I have a feeling I'm going to need all the moral support I can get."

"How are things going between you two? I can't pull any information out of her."

"Truthfully? It's like a piece of me was missing, and now I found it. I love her."

I was happy for them, but part of me was a little jealous.

"I'm glad. You know how highly I think of her. She's basically my sister."

"I know. Thanks for being friends with her. Who knows if we would have ever met otherwise?"

"Anytime, big brother. Anytime."

I told him to call me when he was ready to confront Dad and Mother.

Chapter 31

Evan

I tried to get Ace to understand the deal about the inheritance thing, but he wasn't trying to hear that. Evidently he'd been burned by someone who never paid him a while back, and he wasn't going to go out like a punk again.

I started contemplating whether I should just go forward and do the deed myself, but I couldn't imagine myself as a killer. Plus, I kept hearing my mama's voice in my head telling me I know what's right and I should do right.

I got all that, but I was trying to do right and this was where it got me—involved in a rich stripper's plan to kill her fuckin' father. I went back to thinking about Rocky again and how small of a world this motherfucka really is. I still couldn't believe Rocky would set out to steal another chick's dude, though. Wasn't her style.

I started thinking that it was probably best that Ace wasn't going to go through with the plan. I had started having nightmares about going back to jail and even waking up in a room of fire. I think God or my mama was trying to tell me something, and when one or the other of those two talked, you do best to listen.

I decided that I didn't want to be blamed in any way, shape or form, so I decided to call in an anonymous tip to the police. I couldn't even be associated with anything like what almost went down. I was still being watched.

"I want to report someone for conspiring to commit murder."

"One moment, please."

"Detective Greg Frame speaking."

"Detective Frame, Catalina Richards is trying to hire a hit man to kill her father, Jim Richards of Mitchellville. I don't have any other information, except that money is the motivation."

"And your name, Mr.—"

I hung up.

I called my brother that night. His wife answered the phone and I heard them arguing for a few seconds before he came to the phone. I told him I was sorry for everything and he started to soften up.

We talked about Mama for a while and he admitted that he was hurt when she left the house to me. I told him everything that had happened in the last few weeks, and he actually told me he was proud of me for doing the right thing.

"So what now?" he asked.

"I don't know. I feel like I need to get up out of DC. Too much shit here."

"You could come here. I'm always needing skilled mechanics."

"For real? But, nah, I wouldn't want to impose on you and your family."

"E, you are family."

I think that was the nicest thing he ever said to me. I told him I'd think about it and get back with him in a week or so.

My mind was already made up, though. Without Rocky and my mama, there was nothing left for me in DC.

Chapter 32

Layla

Sierra called me and said we to have a serious talk. I was a little excited to get together with her again, so I went over to her place wearing a long black trench coat and stilettos. Once she closed the door, I opened the trench, revealing nothing but my naked body. "Please close that." She nodded to the jacket belt.

I pressed my finger to her lips and started moving my hips back and forth in a teasing motion.

I could tell it was turning her on. Her complexion was getting slightly rosy under its normal golden tone.

I moved closer to her and placed her hands inside the open trench to caress my hard nipples. "You see how bad I want you?" I moved her and down between my thighs so she could feel the wetness she'd generated.

"Ummm," she moaned. Then she sat down with her elbows on her knees and her head in her hands.

"What? What's wrong? I thought you'd like it."

"That's not why I called you here."

"Oh."

"Layla, I can't do this anymore."

"This?"

"I need more. Sex isn't enough anymore, and I know that's all you're willing to give. You demonstrated that when you left me alone in my bed both times. You showed me that when you never contacted me unless it was for sex."

I was stunned. I slowly walked to the couch and lowered myself. "Wow."

"I know you are exploring your sexuality, but I feel too much for you to allow myself to be your guinea pig."

"I'm sorry," I said. "I'm so sorry. I didn't realize this had gone this far."

"I should be the one apologizing. I kept this up hoping that you'd become ready to have a real relationship with me."

I had become more than a freak in the sheets. I was a borderline player. That wasn't who I was; that wasn't what I was about. I let the sex rule all the other parts of my personality, and I was almost certain that Raquelle would so not approve of that.

"I led you on. You must hate me."

"I could never hate you. I just need to move on to be with someone I can build a life with. I'm tired of the emptiness. I need more."

I took her hand in mine. "Thank you, Sierra."

"Thanks for what?"

"Thank you for teaching me to keep my mind open and to welcome things that I may not have considered."

She just nodded and looked at the door. I think she was ready for me to leave, so I slowly walked to my car, leaving behind one of the sweetest, coolest females I'd ever known.

"I wish it could have turned out differently, Sierra."

Chapter 33

Catalina

If I was going to do something, I had to do it before my mother came back from the dance competition in New York.

Wanting my father dead had turned into so much more than just some cosmetic surgery bills. I did some "research" on one of my father's former associates, named Lynette. She now worked at Lucas's father's firm. I had heard rumors that she was messing around with my father, but I couldn't believe he would stoop so low as to go after such a common woman when he had my mother at home. My attitude on that subject changed after he showed up at Chica's.

Lynette met with me at a small café near Lane & Associates. She didn't know exactly what I was there for, but I could tell she was interested when I mentioned that there would be a $10,000 informational fee in it for her. It was my last major chunk of money, but I had to look at it like an investment in my future.

"Were you ever involved with my father?"

"It really was a long time ago."

"I don't mean to be rude, but could you please just answer the question."

She nodded. "He and I dated for a while here and there. It was actually mostly there. We didn't go out much in the local vicinity."

And we know why.

I found out my father had me down for $20 million in his will. Lynette only knew that because he had also gotten her pregnant, gone through the DNA testing, and written her son into his will as well. We met up again later that night, and she she provided me with pictures and documentation that what she said was true, and I gave her the $10,000.

That $20 million was why I was able to offer someone so much to kill him. I was just steaming that my plan had been placed on hold because some thug got stiffed a time or two.

Evan hadn't returned any of my calls since I told him I wouldn't be able to give him the up-front money he needed to contract the hit. I had to think of another way to come up with the money. As sick as it may sound, I decided to use Lynette's son to get the money from him to pay Evan the retainer to have him killed.

It had been raining all day and finally stopped around dark. I only had one more day before my mother would be coming home. I had to make my move. When I drove up to the house, the front light and a few of the upstairs lights were on. I pulled into the circular driveway behind my father's Infiniti SUV and sat there for a moment trying to collect my thoughts and the documents Lynette had given me.

I went to the door and knocked a few times before ringing the doorbell. There was still no answer. I remembered the hidden key under the flowerpot on the porch and went to get it. I knew my father was either asleep in another part of the house or he had taken the dog out for a walk around the neighborhood since his car was still there.

I walked into the foyer and looked around the sitting area. "Daddy? Are you here?"

I walked back toward the kitchen with my blackmail folder in my arms and malice in my heart. He wasn't there, so I went back toward the front of the house, where the large, winding marble staircase was located.

I walked up the first few steps before sliding on something wet and sticky on the stairs. I looked up to the landing and it appeared that there was a thick liquid coming from there. I couldn't see it until I climbed a few more steps, but I was starting to get nervous and scared.

I bit the bullet and tried to avoid stepping in any more of the liquid, but when I reached the landing and saw my dead father looking up at me with a large gash on his forehead and a strange angle to his neck, I just screamed.

I made my way to the top of the staircase and saw a small puddle of water. I looked up to the ceiling and saw a round water spot. He must have slipped and fallen. I felt strange seeing him dead like that, even though I had been plotting to have him murdered.

Within moments, I head sirens outside. I couldn't remember calling the police, but there was no other explanation for them being there. Thirty seconds later three policemen barged through the door. They looked at me and ran up the steps. They wore dumfounded looks upon their faces, but it didn't take them long to read me my Miranda rights.

"Catalina Richards? You are under arrest for the murder of Jim Richards. You have the right to remain silent . . ."

That was all I heard before the world went dark.

Chapter 34

Lucas

We still hadn't been able to locate Ace and Nikki. I was trying to wait for her to show up before I confronted my parents, but I felt like I couldn't hold it in any longer.

Jay-Ron was reluctant at first. He told me he didn't want to associate with the man who broke his mother's heart, but I was able to convince him that he didn't have to have any kind of relationship with the man, but he could still benefit from having the man's blood in his veins.

He'd been staying with me since his release from the hospital. I didn't want to risk the fact that he could get caught up in the same cycle all over again.

We left a note in the apartment for Nikki to contact us, but we had still heard nothing.

Jay-Ron, Raquelle, and I were on our way to pick up Layla. She hadn't spoken to Dad since the day she walked out of Lane & Associates, and she was a little eager to put him in his place.

Mother answered the door and looked shocked to see the

four of us. She looked at me, then Layla, and then quickly glanced at Raquelle and Jay-Ron.

"What's going on, Lucas?"

"We need to talk, Mother. Dad too."

"He's in his study working on—"

"Get him please."

She turned to head toward the study, and the four of us settled in the dining room, sitting all on one side of the large mahogany table. I wanted us to project a united front.

A few minutes later, I heard my father arguing with my mother about disturbing him.

"The children are here. They say they need to discuss something with us," I heard her say.

A moment later, Mother joined us in the dining room and took a seat on the opposite side of the table. My father followed a moment later.

"What is the meaning of this? I'm working on important business." He took a seat next to my mother, his brow furrowed. When he saw Jay-Ron sitting there, his face transformed into a mask of disbelief.

"Dad, this is Jay-Ron Jenkins. He's one of my students."

"Nice, uh, to meet you." He tried to focus his gaze elsewhere, but like a magnet, his eye repeatedly returned to Jay-Ron's face.

"Likewise," Jay-Ron mumbled, his eyes fixated on the table surface.

"Now, son, what is so important?" my mother asked.

"I just wanted to tell you a story."

I looked at Raquelle and she squeezed my hand. Layla nodded.

"It's a story about a young man from Southeast. He was a smart young man, and despite the circumstances he was raised in, he did well in school and went on to college and to open his own business."

My father looked like he was going to faint. My mother listened intently.

"Anyway, he met a very rich young woman one day. He knew her parents would never approve of her associating with a young man from the other side of the tracks, so using his imagination, he told them he was from an affluent family but that his parents had died tragically. In fact, this young man was already married to a girl from his neighborhood, but when he met the rich girl, he saw it as a chance for a better life. He ended up divorcing his old sweetheart and marrying the rich girl. They had two children together and continued to live the life of a happy couple."

My mother cleared her throat. "I know what this is about. How dare you bring this bastard in my home?"

You could hear a pin drop at that moment. There I was, thinking I was going to be exposing my father for the asshole he was, and my mother seemed to know the story already.

"Minerva," my father said. "Shut your mouth, woman."

"No. I won't shut it any longer. Yes, Lucas. Your father kept on with that woman after we were married. I know about her bastard children."

She threw an icy glare at Jay-Ron, who sat there in stunned silence. In fact, we were all stunned.

"As a matter of fact, the girl, Nicole, was it? She came here to try to get money from us after the bitch died. I gave her some and told her never to darken our doorstep again, but she kept coming back for more."

Jay-Ron stood up and yelled, "You bitch! You watch your mouth when you talk about my mother."

Dad's voice boomed, "Sit down and shut up, young man.

Minerva, shut up." He turned to me. "Son, you can't possibly understand my story. You grew up in privilege. You couldn't comprehend what it was like to grow up in that hell hole."

"I do." Jay-Ron glared at my father. "And so did my mother. Do you know she waited for you to come back for us? Do you know you broke her heart?"

My father looked wounded. "I know." He returned his attention to me. "What is it that you want, Son? Just what is it that you are trying to do here?"

"I want Nikki and Jay-Ron to have the opportunities we had. I want you to own up to your indiscretions."

"Whatever you want, son." He got up from the table. "Minerva, see to it that they are taken care of." Then he returned to his study and slammed the door.

Layla spoke up then, "Mother, why? Why did you let him hoodwink you like that?"

Mother looked like she would break at any moment. "I loved him, Layla. I would have done anything to keep him with me."

"I can't take this," Layla said. She stormed toward the front door.

I heard her say, "They're in there. What the hell? Go ahead in."

A young woman who resembled Layla and Ace walked into the dining room. My mother's face went completely pale.

"Nikki?" Jay-Ron stood up.

The young girl ignored Jay-Ron. She looked at my mother and said, "We need to talk. I need some more payment."

A morbid thought occurred to me at that instant. "Wait, Mother. What do you mean anything?"

The crying ensued then. "Oh, God. What have I done? What have I done?"

"What? What did you do?"

She continued her frenzy and looked at Jay-Ron. "I'm sorry. I'm so sorry."

"You stupid bitch. Shut up! Shut your mouth." Nikki took off out the door, and we all sat there in stunned silence.

Epilogue

One Year Later

Layla

It's still strange to say, but my mother was a murderer. She confessed to us that day that she had paid Nikki to poison Yasmeen Jenkins. Apparently Nikki didn't get the entire amount of money she was promised, and that was why she came looking for it. My mother said she had been after her for years to get the money.

It was an eerie parallel to Catalina, Lucas, and Raquelle. But I guess you know what they say about history repeating itself. Sometimes I have visions of the my mother and Catalina in prison together, implementing their own class system.

Catalina's mother was shocked when her daughter was incarcerated. I found out from Sierra that her father had cut her off and that was what led her to murder. It's sad what people will do to keep from getting their hands dirty.

In the past year, Raquelle and I have expanded Freak in the Sheets to Philly and Richmond. We plan to open a New York location as well. Sierra moved to New York shortly after our last meeting. I assume she is using her fashion knowledge successfully in the fashion capital of the country.

Raquelle and Lucas are getting married in the fall, and I never thought I would say it, but Raquelle is having a baby. She's excited, but not as much as Lucas. Raquelle says she'll be able to teach sex and pregnancy classes.

Jay-Ron is living with them, and he's thriving at a performing arts school. He's been hired to do some studio work, and he's already passed Lucas up on the piano. Nikki took off somewhere with Ace, and we haven't heard much from her since. I know what she did was wrong, but I still feel bad for her. After all, she is my sister. Jay-Ron doesn't allow us to speak her name in his presence.

Raquelle said Evan called her from Ohio to tell her he had moved. I still didn't think he was a bad guy; he just wasn't able to get in the way of what Raquelle felt for my brother.

Jabar and I are officially together. He's finishing up his degree this summer. Raquelle is trying to recruit him to work at Freak in the Sheets. I'm in love with him, and I know this time it's real and much deeper than the superficial union Hunter and I shared. I realized after everything that went on that sex should be fun, but it's so much better when it's connected with love. Jabar and I have great sex, and it's even better because of the emotions involved. He's been hinting about getting engaged, but I'm happy with where we are. I still think about those sexcapades with Nina and Sierra. Part of me wonders if I've gotten the girl-on-girl thing out of my system.

If Raquelle has ever taught me anything, it's that the ideal woman is a lady in the streets and a freak in the sheets. You just have to know where the boundaries are.

SNEAK PREVIEW OF

SexxxFessions:
Confessions of An Anonymous Stripper

A Novel By

ANDREA BLACKSTONE

1
BAD GIRLS

"He's at it again. This is just so absurd and I'm more than tired of this shit. I swear I feel like giving up on my marriage. It if weren't for our two kids and our financial obligations together, we might not be having this conversation," I said to my sister as I washed dishes. I gazed blankly at my daughter's swing set that was positioned so that I could see her play, when I looked out of the window, on many days like this.

"He's at what again, Mystique?" Ayanna asked.

"I know it's not good to discuss personal relationship issues with relatives, but I have to talk to someone about what's really been going on between me and Donavan. I know you're busy but I called you over here to talk because I'm tired of covering his dirt up. There are those fleeting moments when I still feel close to him, but most of the time he doesn't keep his promises, Ayanna, and he treats me like a stranger. When I call his cell phone I either get his voice-mail or I hear that thumping music in the background. He tells me one thing then comes creeping home four A.M. Things have really gotten out of hand around here," I commented as I held a plate in my hand and looked out of the window.

"Where does he go? What do you think he's doing?" Ayanna asked, bombarding me with questions.

"I don't know what he finds so fascinating about running the streets, but that's all he seems to go when he gets off of work. If he's not hanging out at those damn strip clubs, he's usually at some bar with his boys. I can't speak beyond that. If I had a dime every time the kids ask where's daddy, I'd be rich! All I do is pick up after the kids, help with homework, wash clothes, dishes, drive to ballet class and football practice, and go to work." My eyes began to tear up and my voice began to crack. "Even at work I get treated like crap. My boss just moved me to a smaller office with no windows. I'm stuck in a little box typing legal memos all day, ninety words a minute. My husband doesn't care how hard I work in our home and out. Hell, he used to send me flowers at the job from time to time. These days, he just doesn't seem to notice me. I don't even get a good morning or good night. He's sleeping on the couch downstairs after he comes in. I hate strippers. They're ruining my marriage! It just hurts, Yana," I said, feeling my eyes begin to water. I broke my gaze, grabbed a red and white checkered dishtowel, and began drying the dishes.

"You've got your exotic dancers and you've got your strippers. Some have class, some don't. Don't group everyone together though. You know better than that. Everyone who dances for dollars isn't bad. Your husband is to blame for not paying you enough attention, not the strippers," Ayanna reasoned.

"You're right. He's to blame, too. But I don't appreciate him taking money out of my household to spend it on greedy whores with no morals. Why do they wreck homes like this, and what do these women have that I don't? OK, maybe my body isn't perfect after the two babies. I have gained a little weight."

"That's nonsense, Mystique—you look great and there's nothing wrong with you. You filled out in all the right places after having Brian and Brittney. I'd rather be thick as you than slim like me. Boy is it hard for me to get a date with a brother."

"That's sweet of you to say but you're the one with the great figure. Am I so bad looking that he'd pick me over them? What's happening to my marriage? I wish they'd close every one of these whore houses down."

"Leave the dishes alone and turn around and look at me, sis'," Ayanna said. I did finally and sat down.

"My sister began digging in her purse. She handed me a tissue, then hugged me as I cried over my dull marriage. Perhaps I was being a bit emotional, but I was at my wits end. After she released me from her grip she dug in her purse again, then handed me a small book with a palm tree on the outside of it.

"Here—read diary entry number fifteen. Skip past everything else and find that entry."

"I can't, Ayanna—this is far too personal. You've been keeping a diary since you were a kid. You never let anyone read it."

"Well, for the first time, I'm allowing you to. I know you've snooped in it in the past anyway. Don't act like you've never read my dirt."

"Dirt? What dirt? There was nothing good in it back then." I chuckled a little bit. My voice stopped cracking.

"Whatever, your nosey behind was the reason I switched to ones with a key. Just read it before I change my mind, OK?"

I slowly opened my sister's journal and began to read the entry:

Dear Diary,

My life is one big mess and I hate feeling like I'm no longer in control of it. I know my face must look busted—tired, double luggage, and red. Thanks to stress, I bet I look like some hormonally challenged woman who's caught up in a midlife crisis, although I'm only twenty-four years old. I feel like I can barely breathe because I'm stressing so bad about every problem that's on my crowded plate. I just got word that an interview I was looking forward to was cancelled about three hours before it was supposed to take place.

Let me slow down a little and explain myself. After my publishing deal went sour, I immediately began trying to land a job. After sending out a big batch of resumes, someone left a message saying to call back as soon as possible. I did and was called in for an interview. A job in journalism was promised to me and I was ecstatic, to say the least. I thought my worries were over when I was told to come back and fill out human resources paperwork after scheduling an appointment with Ms. Bryson, the individual who is responsible for processing new employees at some little league newspaper called *The U.S. Times*. It's not a top paper to work for but I was looking forward to using the opportunity to become an entry-level reporter as a stepping stone. My intention was to round up some quality clips for my portfolio and then try to step up to a well-known newspaper after milking the opportunity out of a $25,000 a year job.

As instructed by the person who interviewed me, I called the next day to schedule a time to do so, but that's when I couldn't even get anyone on the phone. In fact, voice mail didn't even kick in so I could leave her a message. After my sixth time calling, an employee finally picked up and took a message. When I still didn't receive a call back from Ms. Bryson, a good four hours later, I called back and the same person answered the phone. I guess she grew tired of hearing my voice and finally said that I could talk to her instead. Some twenty something snooty sounding white chick who identified herself as Debbie told me that they weren't hiring at the newspaper. When she told me that my jaw nearly dropped to the floor. I quickly gathered my words and bluntly asked how things could have changed so drastically in the period of one measly day. Debbie started throwing around some smart comments, but the bottom line was that she said it wasn't her decision or Ms. Bryson's. After pressing Debbie to explain herself further she went on to say that the publisher of the newspaper changed his mind about hiring anyone else because he didn't get the money he was supposed to. She also said the current employees may not even be getting paid on time and even her job is unstable. Debbie didn't sound sorry, never apologized on the company's behalf—nothing. This is why it was easy to slam the phone down in her ear then scratch the company off the list of jobs that I'd applied for. Employers really shouldn't play with job seekers like that—it's just wrong, wrong, wrong! And now I suddenly feel the need to officially panic because I'm out of money, duckets, ends, or whatever you want to call it. However you want to put it, *I'm just broke!* I feel like all of the energy has been drained out of my body and a sharp pain is shooting through the middle of my chest like a knife is stabbing me in the middle of it.

My frazzled state of mind had me spilling my guts to the first person that would listen. I still can't believe that I had this conversation with X—someone who's just a friend I've only known about six months—it's just not his place to see me in this shape or listen to me vent and panic. I should've had this talk with the man I'm closest to in life . . . the man I was in an exclusive relationship with for the last two years. Here I am at a crossroad, don't know which way to turn, and David won't even pick up the phone to listen to what I've got to say. Why? He's mad because I sort of took a weeklong trip and wasn't honest about where I went or why. I led him to believe that I wasn't back in town after returning from my last a turnaround book signing in New York. The truth is, after my last few books were sold I began doing odd jobs because I had no more product to sell. In a state of confusion and panic, I jumped from odd job to odd job—flier distribution for two days, walking dogs for three, and participating in a painless market research study for one. I really wasn't forthcoming about my financial dilemma because I simply stopped seeing the need to bare my soul to a man that never spoke of a future with me. After all, I have known David since I was twenty-one years old. Although I love him I still feel like an outsider in his life. As a result, there are some things I keep to myself—no, a lot of things I keep to myself. When I finally was ready to call, I returned to an irate man who accused me of taking a trip out of town to be with another man, then he slipped and confessed he'd been cheating on me anyway. That led me to remove his ass off of speed dial, leave him at least five nasty email messages, and a good sum of long-winded messages on his home and cell phone. I was hurt and felt abandoned. I hadn't cheated on him since we'd become exclusive. I busted my ass as an author to try and show him that I was about something and could bring something to the table in our relationship. That's who I wanted to be with. That's who I wanted to come home to every night. But as the old saying goes . . . that's life.

So now I've got to turn to a friend who is willing to listen to my dilemma. I guess I can't slap a gift horse in the face. At least someone gives a damn about what's happening to me. I'm sure he had better things to do than listen to me rant, rave, and whine about my situation. But instead, he's the one that stared me in the eye from across the kitchen table, trying to advise his confused and ridiculously broke friend. Room temperature water was all I had to offer him, but he sipped it out of that red plastic cup like it was the best shit in the house. I'm not sure why he's sticking by my side like this. Then again, the selfish part of me didn't care so long as someone was there to pay me attention.

"Baby girl, worrying never solves problems. It's time to think this thing through, because you need money and you need it fast. You have three choices to make some cash quickly and under the table."

"What? What are you thinking?"

"How many male friends do you know that want to get with you?"

"Nearly all of them, I guess," I answered flatly as my stomach growled.

"Oh, for real? Is that right? So there's your clientele right there. The solution is right in front of your face, baby girl. Dance for them privately—problem solved."

"I can't do that!" I exclaimed.

"Then just get one who can afford a mistress. Do you know any wealthy mother fuckers?"

"A few. I dated a millionaire and I know some others."

"Damn, it's like that? Okay, be a mistress. Hit them up and tell them you require ten thousand a month. You know what you've got to do. Work them over."

"You're crazy!"

"J-Lo did it. Puffy got in trouble and she dropped his ass. Diana Ross had a kid by that white man. That's what smart women do. One minute Destiny's child was singing about being independent, the next they're singing about can you pay my bills. This is how the game is played, Ayanna. Use your head, here," X said, pointing at his temple.

"If you've missed what I said, I'm not a gold digger."

"Fine. But you better think hard about getting in those pockets while you still can. If I were a good-looking female, I'd do it. When you get a little older men won't be hollering as much. Do you want to be in the same spot next year? Get a man with some money—a sugar daddy. How many do you know that can afford to donate something toward your finances?"

"You know that's not me, X. I've never wanted any man to do anything for me like that. I graduated magna cum laude and I'm supposed to set myself back by relying on my sex appeal to make money?" I snapped.

I felt humiliated that paying my dues with my schooling hadn't paid off. I'd worked so hard by keeping my nose in the books so I wouldn't ever be in a position like this. Even so, there I was.

"All I'm saying is make what you have work for you. You don't want to do it with a stranger, then don't. In case *you* missed it, your friend wants to get with you that way. If you were with me you wouldn't have to struggle to stack paper like this 'cause you'd be straight. You could be dipping shrimp in butter sauce at Red Lobster right now if you wanted to."

"Like you said, we're friends. I don't sleep with my friends. There's a defined line and there are limits. Besides, I'm not a ho, I'm just broke."

"If you don't want a relationship then just let me help you out. It would be a friends with benefits deal, so that wouldn't make you a ho. Take care of just me like that. I'll go to the bank right now and help you out here and there. I'll delete all of those other broads' phone numbers if you say that's what you want to do. I see the potential in you. I know you're a winner. You're smart, good looking, you don't have no kids. And I know that you'd push me in my music career. You're my ideal woman, baby."

"No, X. That's not what I want and not how I want to get it."

"OK—I'm not going to beg you. When you're ready to come to Daddy, I'll be right here waiting." He took a sip of water. "How much are your bills every month?"

I grabbed a pencil and paper and began calculating my expenses. "The garbage collection is $100 every three months. The gas runs about $350. My electric, say $100. My rent is $1,080. My phones and Internet run about $220. Total, I need at least $2,000 a month. That's not counting my $35,000 school loan that's due."

"You've got a lot of financial demands on your back. Sounds like you're gonna need about three jobs to make it out here. That's what I did back in the day to straighten myself out."

I threw down the pencil and rested my head in my left hand. With my right, I nervously began drumming my fingers.

"You know my health isn't that good. I can try, but I can barely get a $10.00 hour job because my resume is screwed up from when I got sick," I said.

"*And* they're going tax you."

"So what am I supposed to do? Medical bills threw me into debt. That's why I already filed bankruptcy once. To top it off, I just got a letter that my disability work ticket expired. My rehabilitation counselor doesn't even want me to work. I don't want to go back on the system, X. I've come so far to rebuild my life and the way they treat you is humiliating. I can't go back to being treated like a second-class citizen over three hundred dollars a month. I don't want to be trapped by the past of poor health and a weak work history, nor do I want to be a burden to my father—he's already helping me keep a roof over my head. He's on a fixed income, and helping me with a place to stay is enough as it is. I feel like I'm just existing these days. I want my life back; I just don't know how to make that happen. I'm getting older and I'm scared about not having a stable career, a home of my own, and some sort of financial security."

"I feel you, but there's no need to panic. Slow down before you give yourself a heart attack. Let me explain something to you. It's not about where you start out in life, but where you finish. Take a deep breath. Come on baby, do it. Fill them lungs up with air and blow it out a few times. You look too stressed. I ain't trying to have you croak on my ass! And stop drumming your fingers—that's annoying as hell!" I followed X's instruction, then he continued. "There, that's better. Like I was saying, you could do something to trick the system by taking control of the situation and getting in the mix."

"What?"

"You know the artist on my album cover?"

"Yeah."

"She was a dime shortie!"

"And?"

"*And* she danced and made that bread. Shortie had her own everything, just from shaking her ass."

"I can't do that!"

"Won't and can't is two different things, so choose the right word," he corrected.

"Stripping isn't dancing, it's just stripping. There's a big difference. A dancer is trained in the *art* of dance," I said with a sigh.

"I know a lawyer who did it to get through law school. Now the sister has her own practice. Some women use it to get ahead, to get what they need. Many a woman in our community has done it because more of us have financial shit going on and no one to help us out. You ain't no better or no worse than any one of them smart sistas who used dancing to their advantage when they found themselves in a similar situation. I'll be honest about it—this is your last option. I don't know what else to tell you. I'm trying to help you find a solution. Treat it like a challenge, not a chore. It's all about your state of mind. For the record, it *is* an art, and it's legal."

"I don't know anything about stripping. I don't even look like the stripper type!"

"I've seen you dance. You can do it and I can help look out for you. That way you'd have your own money. You would make it for yourself and wouldn't have to ask anyone out here for it. Trust me; you could get paid like she did with no problem. Dancing would be easy for you, *and* you'd be an independent contractor. Uncle Sam can't track what you make in a strip club. What can giving it a shot hurt? As long as you know you'll have a roof over your head, the only way you can go with this thing is up. Look, I'm on your side. I want to see you make it because I believe in your writing talent. Your shit can't get much worse than the spot you're in right now," X replied.

He totally missed the point. When I said I couldn't do it, I meant I *really* couldn't do it. I am not secure in my looks, no matter what men say. I see no reason why men would want to watch me flirt in a half-naked state. I considered everything he'd said and then got up from the kitchen table. I didn't know where I was going—I just felt the need to get up just for the sake of moving.

"Put a CD in. Let me be the judge of if you can dance or not. I'll tell you, honestly."

"No. I don't want to think about this anymore," I insisted.

X got up and opened my refrigerator. "Come on now. All you've got is some lettuce and a bony, rotting roaster chicken that you need to throw out." X closed the fridge, then opened and closed my pantry cabinet.

"Don't be going through my stuff!" I said, embarrassed that I had no real food. With the exception of one can of tomato paste, that was bare too. He sat back down, paying my outburst no mind. "Damn, you don't got shit to eat in here. What are you going to eat tomorrow or the next day? What are you going to do—pawn your TV? Then what next, your furniture? You can keep going until your place is cleaned out, it still won't fix anything. It'll just buy you food for a very short period of time. You better think about that, plan your next step, and snap out of this pity party of yours. This a cold, cold world, baby. Ain't no one out here give a damn if you live or die just because you stuck to your morals. I been around the block—I ain't stupid. It's about survival out here. You've got to hustle by any means necessary," he added.

"Well I wasn't raised to think that way," I snapped, crossing my arms defensively.

"Me either. But when my parents made me stand on my own two feet like a man I had to go hard. *It's Hard Out Here for a Pimp* from the movie *Hustle and Flow* won an Oscar— that should tell you something, baby. Some people took those lyrics too literally. It's hard out here for anyone on the grind trying to make ends meet legally...and extra hard for people of color. The American system is set up for only a few cracker pimps to live good at the top. The rest of us will stay hoes, out on the block making someone else rich 'til the day we die, if we don't wake up and find a way to take our own slice of the pie. Too many of us don't know how to work to-ward a dream while we work for the man. Understanding this is what drives me to do more. I'm gonna eat *and* I'm gonna get mine in the music industry someday—I don't care what nobody say. Fuck that! No one's gonna throw salt in my game."

After X's reality check I found myself becoming curious. *Could I really be a stripper?* I exited the kitchen and walked into my bedroom. X followed me, sat down on my chaise lounge, and watched me insert a Mariah Carey CD into the CD player. The music came on, but I couldn't move. I stood there stiff as a board.

"I can't do this in front of you. We're friends."

"Come on now—have some fun with it. Loosen up and pretend that I'm a customer. It should be easier in front of me, not more difficult."

"OK. I'll try again." I restarted the song and attempted to get lost in the thumping beat, but I still felt like a quivering mass of jelly. X nodded his head as tried to I let the music pull me into the melodic groove. It was hard though. Everything seemed wrong. It was broad daylight—it's not like I could dim the lights. To cope with my embarrassment, I looked right past him. As awkward as it was, I let him guide me.

"Now slow it down. Move to the beat, but slower. Make it move a little slower," he said giving me a little constructive criticism.

It was like giving instructions to a new lover, explaining what you like and how. Although I was dancing barefoot in a nightie short set without lipstick or heels, it was an erotic experience that I preferred not to have with a friend. What we were doing was for a lover's eyes only.

I followed his instructions until my confidence grew. I started looking him in the eye seductively, like a g-string diva, watching for some type of reaction. He lowered his eyelids, not returning my stare.

"Please watch me while I can let you," I told him half irritated.

"You're ready—you've got the moves. That's what the girls do. Now let's go to a spot and try your luck. You ready?" he asked.

I glanced down at his jeans. He'd obviously gotten hard from watching me sloppily grind and wind. X played it off by taking his hand way from his jeans but I'd already caught him running his hand over his fabric-covered manhood. In an odd way I was flattered.

"No, I'm not X," I told him as the image of a Playboy model type shot through my head.

"Let's go. Stop procrastinating here. You're wasting time, and time is money," X said as he stood and stretched.

"No—I'm staying here."

"You need to put some food on your table, sweetheart. Let's go talk to the manager of some clubs. Now stop being scared. I'm going with you. I'll be right there by your side. I'll look out for you while you're stripping—I promise. I swear on my grandmother's grave," he said, reassuring me.

"I can't. I can't," I insisted.

"You said you don't want to be a burden to your father. The man's not rich, remember?" He paused, letting his words sink in. "Look, it's your decision, but I'm trying to show you a way to get money fast just for shaking your ass and using your looks to get you by until you find a decent job."

"What if someone sees me? If I do become successful one day I can't afford some scandal down the road."

"No one is putting food on your table and paying your bills. All publicity is good publicity. You know I'd never tell, but if anyone ever found out who you are, so what? It'll push up book sales. Them folks will run out to snatch a copy then, 'cause people will know that you're not perfect either. They love dirt and grit—it's a win-win situation for you. I say you got a plan."

"You seem to have the answers for everything, so I'll go ahead and ask. What plan?" I said as I turned off the music.

"To save some money to get your new book out there— write about what you experienced in the strip world. You can get everything you need in one place—money and a damn good story. I always want you to control your product, from now on. That's the key—to control your product yourself.

Only give it up if the big boys come knocking. Until then, keep control. That's what my old man taught me about my music. Call it something scandalous like *Strip Life*. I'll invest in it, but you've got to put something up too. Now listen, I have to go to work soon so you need to let me know what you want to do."

"Let me sleep on it. I'll call you in the morning after I think this whole thing over."

"Suit yourself," he said, shaking his head.

I just got out of bed, even though the sun set a few hours ago. No, it's not because I'm lazy! It's because I didn't actually go to bed until 3:00 a.m. I spent the whole night surfing the net, trying to find jobs to apply for. Interestingly enough, when I googled the word "internships," it led me to an odd place in cyberspace—well maybe not that odd. I happened upon this chick's controversy that I'd heard of in prior years, but I never knew her name or the details. She was a senatorial staffer who apparently had landed an entry-level job in D.C.—on the Hill—slept with politicians, then posted her exploits on the net in a blog she claimed was meant for her friends' eyes only. What a way to spend the government's money though. She was updating her blog while she was at work!

Anyway, after a few weeks of using initials, dropping one-liners, and getting a little drama stirred up in cyberspace, her boss found out and the little naughty vixen was tossed out on (what appears to be) her Amer-asian can. After that, reporters and literary agents blew up her phone like the number was about to change. Now this outspoken college drop out is living "the life." Her punishment for outing fair lawmakers and proponents of morality was a six figure book deal with Hyperion/Disney and getting paid sweetly to pose in *Playboy*, pretending to tap on a laptop, among other things.

In her blog, Cutler asked herself how anyone could make it on $25,000 a year in a city like D.C. Right now, I'd kill for those crumbs! I can't apply for some jobs because they require you have "good credit." Oh well? Maybe if I'd sucked dick on the Hill or let that politician I know (I won't provide his initials) bang me at The Hilton as requested, I wouldn't be writing my version of *The Broke Diaries*.

Cutler blogged for two weeks, landed a book deal, has the producer of *Sex in the City* ready to put her on as a consultant of an HBO show based on her characters, and a bunch of other miscellaneous perks. The point is, as an author, I've been out there a *little* while. Still, Cutler's career carries more weight than mine. It seems like you have to do something extreme or sensational to get a good shot at a book deal. Reality fiction has taken over so much that securing sizable deal seems to boil down to a matter of who has done worse dirt. If I were stripping for—then fucking—politicians, celebrities and others, then naming who they were, then *maybe* there would be a chance of the press beating my door down, too. I don't want to get wrapped up in scandals though, I just want to make a few quick dollars to get by. Obviously, I'm not as bold at the next chick, so why not just strip in secret and call it a day? Sex sells, so hopefully, getting a job in adult entertainment will be easier than it's been for me trying to land one in an office.

Venting about my situation has led me to decide that I'll give X's suggestion a shot. After sleeping on it, I can't help but feel that my options are few. Hell, I asked my father to send me fifty dollars and the check bounced. He said he'd have to move some of his money around to help me any more than he already does. I told him never mind. I can't put him through any more stress. I'm a grown woman who should take responsibility for my fucked up situation. If I really end up making it through an audition, I won't be proud of what I do to get by, and I'd never put my face out there because I did it. I do feel it's morally wrong to take off my clothes for money, despite the fact that it could help keep me fed. So I guess that's one difference between me and "them." I feel guilty about what I'm about to try to do and what I may do. Thus, I'd never reveal who I am to help generate more book buzz—at least not intentionally.

I called X and told him that I've decided to take the plunge. Within ten minutes I was sitting on the passenger's side of X's Hummer. I may be broke, but I have friends on all levels in life. X's first single was doing extremely well in Europe and he was beginning to make some noise in The States. He produces music and raps, but he's also working fulltime until his record gets released. In fact, his manager is busy organizing his first real tour. His finances are in order, even after having gone through some of the same things I'm dealing with, so I respect what he said. He obviously knew how to make and keep money in the bank. I met X at a book signing where I was signing my first title. We became casual friends and made a pact that whomever hit it really big would reach back and help the other one. He hadn't quite made it to the big show yet, but he wasn't about to leave me behind either.

The first stop we made was at a local spot. He opened my door then locked the car. Forget the swanky décor and fancy design schemes they may have in Vegas—this place was anything but glamorous. It looked to be an old fast food restaurant. I could imagine girls piling in cabs to get to what looked to be a blue collar titty bar, or even carpooling to arrive. As we walked toward the old looking structure, I began to feel as if I couldn't swallow properly. X opened the door and confidently walked straight to the bar. A girl who I assume to be a stripper was sitting on a well broken in barstool, playing cards on a computer. The club hadn't opened to customers yet.

"Yeah. She wants to talk to the manager about dancing," X said to someone behind the bar. I looked in the other direction like he had experience inquiring for himself.

"Hey Butch. Someone out here wants to talk to you about dancing," the person yelled over his shoulder. "You can go in the back." He made a motion with his head.

"You said you'd stay with me. Can you come with me?" I asked X under my breath.

"I can't go back there. It will look like I'm your pimp and I'm forcing you to do this. Go ahead. Just tell them you want to audition."

I sighed and left. I opened a door and walked into a cramped, cluttered room. I was told that a man was the day manager, but a woman appeared.

"Hello. I'd like to know about auditioning to dance," I told her. I felt my heart begin to race.

She looked me over. "Oh, they'll like you. They like redbones. Go get your clothes and come right back."

"Do you dance?" I asked her.

"I used to," she admitted. "Are you coming back—do you live far?"

"No, I don't live far. I'll be back soon," I replied.

"OK," she answered. She turned around and walked to-ward a kitchen area and I went to find X. She seemed as if she was eager for me to return. The question was why?

"What did they say?"

"Come back and bring some clothes."

"They want you to dance today, so be prepared."

"You don't know that!" I snapped.

"You'll be dancing tonight. I know what I'm talking about. That's good. It's Friday—you should make some money. Now look, you know you can come back here. Let's go check out a few more spots downtown."

"But I told the lady that I'd come right back."

"You already know you can dance there. That place isn't going anywhere. You got that one on lock."

Fifteen minutes later, X and I were walking into an upscale club. The building was huge and impressive—a little closer to the Vegas fantasy. I could imagine women wearing little black dresses accompanying their beau to get turned on, and high profile men wearing expensive clothes and smoking cigars frequenting this location.

"It's nothing to see dudes with Bentleys and limos roll up here. This is one spot where the high rollers come. If you're rich and you live in this town, you've been through this one. If you're a high-profile celebrity visiting in this town, this is where you come. The bottom line is this is where da the real money's at."

As I looked at the building while X led. I felt like a tourist in a foreign city. Talking about completely green, that was me!

"Come on. I keep telling you that time is money." He strolled in confidently just like before. "Yeah, man. She wants to talk to the manager about dancing," X said to a cleaning man.

"The boss is upstairs. Go on up that way."

X and I walked past a beautiful bar, pink and blue strobe lights, and several large stages. The club was complete with plush couches and many VIP areas. If I were going to dance, this was more my speed.

"Yes?" a woman said.

As she spoke I noticed a small black woman behind her. The pair looked like night and day. One was small and light, and the other big and very dark-skinned.

"I'd like information about dancing," I told her nervously.

She looked at me suspiciously from behind her desk. I sized her up as well. She looked like she loved Twinkies and junk food a bit too much. Then she handed me a white packet of paper.

"Fill this out, copy your driver's license, then bring it back here. If we have any openings, we'll call you," she said without cracking a smile.

"You don't have any openings now?" X asked.

"She can fill out the application," the woman answered.

I began to read it as we left the room. "X, they want far too much personal information. There's no way I'm putting down where I went to high school, if I speak foreign languages, where I went to college, or giving these people a copy of my license. They want to know if they can contact a current employer, if you've ever been in a mental hospital, and even want to swear you'll submit to a polygraph test." I continued reading as we walked. "It's four pages long! There's no way that I'm going to give them all of this information. The point is for me to get this story discreetly, not try and make a career out of this corny shit."

"Just fill it out. You're a writer. Be creative and make something up. They ain't going through the trouble of no polygraph test," he said as he looked at the stage below.

"But they're making you swear it's all true. I'm scared to lie. I don't want to break the law."

"Look, either you do this or you go back to the other spot. You said take you somewhere upscale and I did. What do you want from me? Do you want to dance here or not?" X said in an irritated tone.

"Maybe—I don't know."

"If you want to dance here I'll go back and talk to the woman. You can't be talking like you want information when you want to dance. You didn't talk right. You're messing yourself up," X said shaking his head.

"If you haven't noticed, this is kind of a stressful day for me. I don't know anything about strip life! I told you that," I snapped back.

"Come on, let's go. You can think about it. There's one more spot up the street we can check out."

I stuffed the papers in my junky purse and followed X. He didn't even have to move the car—that's how close the clubs were. I opened the door to the second club. My eyes fell on a pasty colored, aging white man who was sitting in a chair near the door. X told him I wanted to dance.

"How old are you?" he asked.

"Twenty-four," I said.

"Come back later. The manager's name is Mary Ann.

I thanked him and told X what he said. After that, we cruised down the highway so that my road dog could get ready for work.

"Were you paying attention to how we got here?" X asked.

"I don't need to know. I was just getting information!" I snapped.

"I've got to go home, switch cars, and go to work. Go up to the first spot and audition. As far as the other two, we'll follow up on them later. You need to dance in at least two clubs, five times a week to get your paper straight. Keep that in mind."

"I'm not going back to the first club by myself."

"I can't go. I have to go to work. Come on now—just go in the joint and audition. I'll stay on the phone with you up until it's your turn to dance. OK?"

"OK. Fair enough," I agreed.

X dropped me off and I was feeling rather unsure about my plan. I looked everywhere for something to wear and I didn't have many clothes. When it came to something sexy to wear for my man, usually thongs and heels sufficed. I'd seen Demi Moore's *Strip Tease* years ago. I also had this preconceived notion that stripping entailed false eyelashes, gloves, implants, exotic dresses, and tons of wigs. I didn't think that was quite what I was in for, where I lived. The hood isn't Hollywood. The hood is the hood and I didn't want to make a critical error during my audition by looking like the green girl that I am. I was totally confused regarding what to expect—I must've called X four times about me not having real dance clothes. I finally settled on something frilly I was able to squeeze into. It really didn't look like something a stripper would wear but it was all I had. I showered, lotioned, shaved, packed a small bag, and was off to see what I was in for by dusk. After all, it was the twenty-fifth of the month and I had no other way to try and pay my bills by the first.

After I lifted my head and shut Ayanna's diary, I was trying to recover from the shock of learning about my sister's secret life. I couldn't believe that she'd hidden this from me for so long.

"Please don't judge me for what I did, Mystique. I know some people would say I demeaned myself by playing to role of a sex object, but I really don't look at it in such a political light. Obviously, I really needed the money for law school and it's been a way to help me get it. With Mom dead and all, I couldn't burden Dad any more than he already has been."

"I had no idea you were going through all of that. I thought your little ghetto book was doing well. I saw for sale it all over the place."

"It was—I just didn't get the money for it. I planned to use my royalties to help tie me over. The bad part began when I ran out of books. I didn't have $5,000 for another print run and I was getting many requests for it. As a novice, I needed guidance and an investor. So, a so-called friend of a friend who had a little loot agreed to finance one print run. A ten percent cut doesn't go very far after *three* or so printings. It turned out that many more copies of my book were printed than I was aware of. Let's just say that I ended up buying more books back over and above the person's initial investment, and I was contractually confined to the agreement. I knew that I couldn't keep that up, and when a deal was struck with a small publisher, my hands were tied since my investor didn't want me to move on with the project. As a result, I was stuck in a bind that would keep me standing in a deep hole. Having no royalty payment for the whole year led me to hit rock bottom and linger down in the dumps. I was unemployed, but ineligible for unemployment, well . . . traditional employment that is. Plus, I owed my lawyer two thousand dollars for the work she'd done to try and get me released from the agreement and to file a copyright infringement charge. How was I going to have money to drive to job interviews, feed myself, and pay my bills until some of the clouds lifted and someone put me on their payroll?"

"I know that's right," I commented, feeling Ayanna's pain.

"All of this was up in the air, until my streetwise friend X paid me a visit. I decided not to shop my story to a publisher though. They're looking for unusual memoirs, street fiction, and hip hop lit from new talent. I don't think my circumstance is interesting enough to be worth the trouble. I decided to just keep my typical day-to-day stuff to myself, although between these pages. School keeps me busy enough anyway. I'm over the book fiasco—you win some, you lose some. Just like they say, what don't kill you will make you stronger."

"Why didn't you ask me for help? I may have been able to get you some legal advice at a discount. There was no need for you to struggle that way. And you should never give up on your writing—you have real talent."

"I wasn't going to put you in the position of asking for any favors at work. I know how they are. Most artists get ripped off the first time around. Now that someone tore me a new asshole, I realize that I'd rather be a lawyer than a writer. I can't be a starving artist—I just don't have it in me. Since I never did find a professional job, that's the real reason that I decided to go back to school. If fate is kind, I'll be a lawyer by this time next year. If I have my way I'll go into private practice and we can work together. Your boss treats you like shit and you do all the hard work at that firm. In fact, you need to get your props officially and at least get your paralegal credentials. You already do a paralegal's work anyway."

"Thanks, Yana. As you know, I just do it for the money. I hate my job, but a good check is good a check. Anytime you need help, just ask. You should've said something. I'm your big sister, remember? I may be married but I'll never stop sharing. You've been such a good little sister. Whatever happens in life, I'll be right there with you through it all."

"Thanks, boo. I couldn't burden you like that though. You know how independent I am."

"Well at you started dancing for a good reason and a specific purpose. I know you can accomplish anything. I'll be the first one cheering my sis' on when she gets that J.D." I smiled.

"Sisters forever?" Ayanna said.

"Sisters—this is just between us," I replied.

"Thanks. You're the best. I sort of feel better that it's off my chest, but you still looked stressed. I wasn't going to say anything but you always look tired and unhappy. I love the kids but I'm glad they're at camp. If anyone ever needed a break, it would be you."

"I'm just a married old hag. It's my job to be stressed." I sighed.

"I have an idea," Ayanna said, her eyes lighting up.

"What?"

"Don't sit around moping, and don't get mad with the old ball and chain, get *even*! Take that Leave It To Beaver's mother apron off, put some lipstick on those lips, and for the love of God, change those ugly shoes! You're going out to get some air and I won't take no for an answer. I insist and you know how I am once I make up my mind, so you may as well just give in."

After I spruced myself up a little, Ayanna drove me to the club where she worked. The joint was the kind of neighborhood strip club where there is no head doorman or champagne rooms. The places I'm referring to is the type that could be found in basements of buildings, abandoned shopping centers, or old fast food restaurants. These bad neighborhoods are populated by all the makings of a ghetto: a greasy spoon fast food Chinese place, a liquor store, an overpriced grocery store, and a tennis shoe pit stop. There are no cleaners, no watering holes, deli cafes, or banks. You must have a good picture of what I'm referring to now . . . *certainly.*

She found a table near the main stage and ordered me to sit down. Never having been in a strip club before, I looked all around as best I could, considering the lighting was dim as dim could be, except for the stage area. After Ayanna finished greeting a few people she returned to the table and sat across from me.

"Yana, what am I doing here?" I asked, looking around with a sweeping glance.

"You're making me crazy. Shut up and order a drink. It's on me. What do you want? The waitress doesn't have all day," she teased.

"Bottled water and lemon please," I told the woman.

"Don't listen to her. She'll have Patron and I'll have Hypnotiq. No, scratch that. That'll be bottled water for me. Thanks, T," Ayanna said with a smile.

After ordering drinks, I expected to watch the girls dance, but it was still a bit early.

"Hey, wanna have some fun?" Ayanna asked.

"How?" I asked, sounding baffled.

"I dare you to go up there. I double dog dare you," she told me with a big ole grin.

"Up where?" I asked.

"On stage, fool. See how it feels."

"Are you crazy, Ayanna? All that studying has knocked the good sense of out your head. I don't think so," I replied, shaking my head no from side to side.

"No one's here yet. You can even keep your clothes on. I already asked the manger if it would be all right—he said it was fine. Hurry up before the girls come out. They're getting dressed in the back right now. Don't be so self-conscious, come on!"

"I can't. I already told you that," I snapped.

"I dare you—come on, it's fun!" Ayanna insisted, tugging at my arm.

"How childish," I snorted.

"Your problem is that you don't know how to let go. You act like it costs you something to laugh. You're so conservative—you need to take the stick out of your asshole and loosen up."

"Ayanna! Watch your language!" I scolded. "And I am not too conservative."

"You've always been an introvert that acted as if you were carrying the weight of the world on your shoulders. Mystique, that's just no good."

"That's because I've always had a lot of responsibilities—including helping Dad raise you," I defended.

"When's the last time you had some fun?" Ayanna said, ignoring my comment.

"Fun?" I repeated as if it were a foreign word.

"I feel for you. See what I'm saying? You are too uptight. You've been around those anal attorneys at the firm too long. You know, the ones I bet make the most terrible lovers," she told me, waving her hand. "Whatever you do, don't lose your sense of humor in life. Embrace the funk and feel good all over anyway! That's what I learned and what's gotten me over this hump. I have to laugh to keep from crying. Try it, you may like it."

"You never cease to amaze me, you crazy fool," I told my sister, cracking a slight smile.

I found myself walking toward the stage and no longer cared if anyone was watching our silly behavior. Ayanna giggled and dropped a quarter in a jute box near the stage. When she did, she walked up on stage with me and persuaded me to try and follow her movements as we listened to T-Pain's hot new joint, *U and Dat.* There I stood in my jeans, struggling for my eyes to adapt to the glow of the light, getting a crash course in pole dancing from my baby sister. Ayanna had always been a natural actress and often turned out to be the center of attention. She appeared to be completely comfortable with her sexuality, swaying her hips while making sexy gestures in public. Part of me envied Ayanna— I found myself wanting to feel the very same way.

"See, you feel better, right?" Ayanna asked, continuing to move around.

"Don't I look like it?" I commented, gripping the pole with both hands, then slowly rising back up. When I reached the top I alternated kicking my legs out, pointing my toes.

"You go gurl!" she said. Half laughing, I high-fived Ayanna, then poorly mimicked her crazy moves as T-Pain belted out a mouthful of explicit but sexy words.

After two songs, Ayanna pulled my hand, giggling. We walked off the stage and sat in our seats as the girls began day shift for the lunch crowd. By that time the waitress had come with our drinks. Since my sister was driving, I finished sipping my drink and shamelessly watched the girls strip as they dug in their toolbox of tricks. I gulped hard and blushed when the first one removed her top, then exposed her breasts and dropped her shimmering thong, while staring directly into my eyes. But when the second one made smoke ooze from the amber glow, as she took drags of a cigarette with her pussy, my eyes were glued to the stage like a child to a circus act. Ayanna laughed at the trick that I'm sure she'd seen before, but I was just plain stunned and amazed. Things were winding down when the theatrics ended. I enjoyed watching the dancers that followed tease and charm customers with their sensuous pole twirling moves. They didn't seem as interested in topping the next girl with odd talents—their beauty was enough to hook men alone. I found myself wishing that I had the guts to tip them myself, when a steady stream of men showed them some love, but I didn't.

As each song played, and each dancer seemed to offer something different, I reflected back on her story and wondered if I could secretly be a stripper too. My sister didn't know it, but just standing up on stage under those lights gave me a rush of excitement I couldn't shake, and watching other women work their bodies right as men sipped beer around us only heightened my curiosity. More than that, the drink loosened me up, my shoulders relaxed, and my pussy was dripping wet.

Ayanna and I grew up in a quiet, sleepy town with a small population, where people still believe in good old fashion values. Our parents taught us to always say please and thank you, and we were reared in a home that was so conservative that I was grounded just for asking to try out for the high school cheerleading squad. We attended prestigious prep schools and universities that are normally reserved for girls named Buffy and Samantha, and also attended Bible School when we were growing up. I rarely use slang and Ayanna is still learning how to sling it like she's cool and confident. For reasons I won't mention, we know what cow tipping is, and once knew as many Garth Brooks, Stylistics, and Gloria Estefan songs as Fifty and Snoop. That's why I found it hard to believe that Miss Ayanna gave the strip scene a whirl in a place like where we were seated. From what I saw that day, if you don't take it all off before you step off that stage when your set ends, you don't get tipped.

Although I was married with children, at the time I wanted to spread my wings and fly like a carefree bird. For the first time in years, I felt that my world didn't revolve around Donavan or my two kids. I somehow managed to find myself craving liberation and adventure. Coupled with the unchartered territory of urban life, I was intrigued by exotic dancing, stripping, or however you want to put it. In fact, with the kids away at camp, I even planned to take the week off as I fantasized about being a bad girl. Instead of being too scared to ever return to a place like the Foxy Lady, that was the beginning of the day that I declared that I'd say goodbye to bad love, and hello to the notion of unleashing the freak within by getting paid to show off. Just like my husband, I wanted to have a good time. All work and no play had made Mystique a very boring girl. I needed some me time and I had a feeling that I was about to get it while exploring my adventurous side.

ABOUT THE AUTHOR

MadameK is an avid reader and music connoisseur. She has a library that exceeds over 5000 books. She lives in the suburbs where she tries to find quiet time to read, write, and relax.

She's currently working on her second novel, due out in September 2008.

LOOK FOR MORE HOT TITLES FROM

Q-BORO
B O O K S

DARK KARMA - JUNE 2007
$14.95
ISBN 1-933967-12-9

What if the criminal was forced to live the horror that they caused? The drug dealer finds himself in the body of the drug addict and he suffers through the withdrawals, living on the street, the beatings, the rapes and the hunger. The thief steals the rent money and becomes the victim that finds herself living on the street and running for her life and the murderer becomes the victim's father and he deals with the death of a son and a grieving mother.

GET MONEY CHICKS - SEPTEMBER 2007
$14.95
ISBN 1-933967-17-X

For Mina, Shanna, and Karen, using what they had to get what they wanted was always an option. Best friends since day one, they always had a thing for the hottest gear, luxurious lifestyles, and the ballers who made it all possible. All of this changes for Mina when a tragedy makes her open her eyes to the way she's living. Peer pressure and loyalty to her girls collide with her own morality, sending Mina into a no-win situation.

AFTER-HOURS GIRLS - AUGUST 2007
$14.95
ISBN 1-933967-16-1

Take part in this tale of two best friends, Lisa and Tosha, as they stalk the nightclubs and after-hours joints of Detroit searching for excitement, money, and temporary companionship. These two divas stand tall until the unforgivable Motown streets catch up to them. One must fall. You, the reader, decide which.

THE LAST CHANCE - OCTOBER 2007
$14.95
ISBN 1-933967-22-6

Running their L.A. casino has been rewarding for Luke Chance and his three brothers. But recently it seems like everyone is trying to get a piece of the pie. An impending hostile takeover of their casino could leave them penniless and possibly dead. That is, until their sister Keilah Chance comes home for a short visit. Keilah is not only beautiful, but she also can be ruthless. Will the Chance family be able to protect their family dynasty?

Traci must find a way to complete her journey out of her first and only failed

LOOK FOR MORE HOT TITLES FROM

Q-BORO BOOKS

NYMPHO - MAY 2007
$14.95
ISBN 1933967102
How will signing up to live a promiscuous double-life destroy everything that's at stake in the lives of two close couples? Take a journey into Leslie's secret world and prepare for a twisted, erotic experience.

FREAK IN THE SHEETS - SEPTEMBER 2007
$14.95
ISBN 1933967196
Librarian Raquelle decides to put her knowledge of sexuality to use and open up a "freak" school, teaching men and women how to please their lovers beyond belief while enjoying themselves in the process. But trouble brews when a surprise pupil shows up and everything Raquelle has worked for comes under fire.

LIAR, LIAR - JUNE 2007
$14.95
ISBN 1933967110

Stormy calls off her wedding to Camden when she learns he's cheating with a male church member. However, after being convinced that Camden has been delivered from his demons, she proceeds with the wedding.

Will Stormy and Camden survive scandal, lies and deceit?

HEAVEN SENT - AUGUST 2007
$14.95
ISBN 1933967188
Eve is a recovering drug addict who has no intentions of staying clean until she meets Reverend Washington, a newly widowed man with three children. Secrets are uncovered that threaten Eve's new life with her new family and has everyone asking if Eve was *Heaven Sent*.

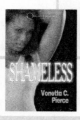
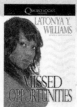
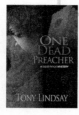

Attention Writers:

Writers looking to get their books published can view our submission guidelines by visiting our website at: *www.QBOROBOOKS.com*

What we're looking for: Contemporary fiction in the tradition of Darrien Lee, Carl Weber, Anna J., Zane, Mary B. Morrison, Noire, Lolita Files, etc; groundbreaking mainstream contemporary fiction.

We prefer email submissions to: submissions@qborobooks.com in MS Word, PDF, or rtf format only. However, if you wish to send the submission via snail mail, you can send it to:

Q-BORO BOOKS Acquisitions Department
165-41A Baisley Blvd., Suite 4. Mall #1
Jamaica, New York 11434

*** By submitting your work to Q-Boro Books, you agree to hold Q-Boro books harmless and not liable for publishing similar works as yours that we may already be considering or may consider in the future. ***

1. Submissions will not be returned.
2. **Do not contact us for status updates.** If we are interested in receiving your full manuscript, we will contact you via email or telephone.
3. Do not submit if the entire manuscript is not complete.

Due to the heavy volume of submissions, if these requirements are not followed, we will not be able to process your submission.